## "They all think you're sweet, don't they?" Michael murmured

"Everyone assumes you're just a good girl who does what she's supposed to."

"I am." Tate smiled as she snuggled against his lean hard body.

"Hmm... I overheard your discussion of *Story of O*, remember? And I know *exactly* how you feel about that steamy scene in *The Big Easy*. You might have been on the phone with Sara, but you were really talking to me."

"Oh, God," she said, burying her head in the pillow so he couldn't see her blush. "Was I that obvious?"

"Yes. You were." He was grin

It was just the k........... in her bed, alone, i............... m was perfect. The............ something out o............ for the danger th......... a whisper away.

She groaned.

"Hey, I liked it. I like you."

Tate shook her head, not wanting to believe. She knew he was just trying to distract her so she wouldn't be scared.

He leaned down so his mouth was close to her ear. "I used to go home and stroke myself to the memory of your sexy voice...."

# Blaze™

Dear Reader,

This is so politically *uncorrect* it's embarrassing to admit: I've had kidnap fantasies since I was about twelve. I saw a movie back then where a young woman was kidnapped and it set my imagination on fire. I don't remember the name of the movie, or much else about it, just that there was something about being stolen, being taken away from all I knew that intrigued and excited me.

So it was with great anticipation and a little evil glee that I set about writing Michael and Tate's story for the FORBIDDEN FANTASIES miniseries. In so many ways this book is the essence of fantasies that have been with me for years. But it was only as I finished the book that I realized in all my dreams, in all my late-night visions, the outcome was always, always...*love*.

Come visit me at www.joleigh.com.

Sweet dreams,

*Jo Leigh*

# JO LEIGH
## Kidnapped!

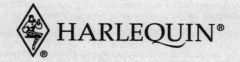

TORONTO • NEW YORK • LONDON
AMSTERDAM • PARIS • SYDNEY • HAMBURG
STOCKHOLM • ATHENS • TOKYO • MILAN • MADRID
PRAGUE • WARSAW • BUDAPEST • AUCKLAND

ISBN-13: 978-0-373-79349-5
ISBN-10:     0-373-79349-9

KIDNAPPED!

## ABOUT THE AUTHOR

Jo Leigh has written more than thirty books for Harlequin and Silhouette Books since 1994. She's a triple RITA® Award finalist, most recently receiving a nomination from the Romance Writers of America for her Harlequin Blaze novel, *Relentless*. She also teaches writing in workshops across the country.

Jo lives in Utah with her wonderful husband and their cute puppy, Jessie. You can chat with her at her Web site, www.joleigh.com, and don't forget to check out her daily blog!

## Books by Jo Leigh
### HARLEQUIN BLAZE

*In Too Deep...

To LWW.
Because he's better than the fantasy.

# 1

It was Tuesday at one-fifteen in the afternoon, and with the precision of a Swiss watch Tate Baxter's therapist leaned back in her chair, closed her notebook, smiled, then said, "Is there anything else you'd like to tell me?"

Tate's response was just as mechanical. "No, Dr. Bay. Nothing to report."

"Well, I have something I'd like to show you."

Tate lifted her head. One-fifteen was the end of the session. Dr. Bay never went over. Never. "Oh?"

The doctor flipped her notebook over and pulled out a newspaper article. "Take a look at this," she said.

Tate took the paper, torn between reading the article and watching Dr. Bay. The therapist, whom Tate had been seeing for almost two years, was clearly excited. That hardly ever happened. In fact, it never had. Not like this. Dr. Bay was a behaviorist, always setting up new challenges and goals for Tate to accomplish between sessions. The outcome never elicited anything but a favorable reaction, no matter the performance. Even when Tate had surpassed her own expectations, the doctor had always been reserved. But now Dr. Bay's eyes were wide with anticipation and her pale cheeks looked flushed.

Tate glanced down and the headline sent her own pulse racing. *Kidnapping For Hire.* She looked back at Dr. Bay.

"It's all right, Tate. Please, read it."

After a moment of hesitation, Tate started reading.

It begins with a list of your wildest fears. For a few thousand dollars Jerry Brody's personalized kidnapping service will make them come true. Your kidnappers might stuff you into a duffel bag or blindfold you and take you to a faraway cabin. In the dark you might see an alien's mask or a man in a filthy suit stinking like a garbage Dumpster. No two abductions are staged the same way. Your custom kidnapping could stop at a code word or go on for days. Brody and his team might snatch you when you're on the subway or showering in your apartment. After the "event," which some clients compare to meditation, you may feel relief, exhilaration or a newfound sense of personal power.

Tate had to stop. She'd come a long way since she'd first told Dr. Bay about her kidnap phobia and she hadn't had a full-blown panic attack in months. But this? This was—

"Breathe, Tate," Dr. Bay said. "Remember what we've practiced."

Closing her eyes, she went to her safe space. After several deep breaths, she focused on each part of her body from her toes to the top of her head.

"You're safe. You're in my office and no one's going to hurt you. Picture the glade."

Tate followed Dr. Bay's instructions. By the time she'd finished the awareness exercise she had regained her equilibrium. Her eyes opened to the security of the familiar—and the disappointment that she was still, after so much work, at the mercy of her fears.

"Do you want to talk about this now?" Dr. Bay asked, gesturing at the paper still in Tate's hand.

"You want me to hire this man? To let him take me?"

"I want you to think about it. I've been researching this approach for a long time now and I've spoken to a number of colleagues who have used similar techniques. There are reliable case studies where the subjects have been transformed. But remember, it's simply an idea. You're doing very well following the course we're on, and I realize this is unconventional."

Tate winced at the understatement. She could barely imagine what her father would say about this "unconventional" approach.

"When you go home tonight, I'd like you to do some work in your journal. Not about your reaction to the article but about what your life might be like if you could overcome this fear. Okay?"

Tate nodded. "I'll try."

"That's all anyone can ask. For what it's worth, you did a great job of calming down. It didn't take long at all."

Tate glanced at her watch. It was a quarter to two. Not bad, considering. It hadn't been that long ago that even the suggestion of something like this would have put her in a panic for days.

She put the article on the side table and grabbed her purse. "I'll see you next week."

"Don't forget to meditate."

She never did. And it had helped. She went out more frequently these days, and the nightmares weren't plaguing her nearly as often. Three cheers for the safe place. If only it could exist somewhere outside of her head.

As she was leaving, she nodded at Stephanie, Dr. Bay's receptionist. There were two people in the waiting room, both of whom appeared perfectly normal. She imagined they thought the same thing about her.

There was no one in the elevator as she stepped in, and she took a moment to push her hair back behind her shoulders, to daub the corners of her mouth, preparing herself for the streets of Manhattan.

Not that she would be on the streets—unless one counted being driven in one of her father's black limousines. The tinted windows hid her from view, making her feel as if the city was one giant store display.

The elevator slowed at the fourth floor. She inched back as a man entered. He was tall and silver-haired, wearing a tailored black pin-striped suit. His shoes looked equally expensive, and when he smiled she could see his veneered teeth had cost him a pretty penny. Not surprising, given the address. Dr. Bay's office overlooked Park Avenue. Her clients all understood, even before the first session, that if they had to ask about the fee, they couldn't afford it.

The man turned to stare at the elevator doors as they

rode the rest of the way to the lobby. Only, the doors were reflective and he clearly had no qualms about giving her a very thorough once-over.

She counted the seconds until they reached the lobby, and when the doors slid slowly open she placed her hand strategically so the elevator couldn't be fetched, waiting until the man was halfway across the lobby before she stepped out.

What would her life be like if she stopped being afraid? She had no idea. It was too foreign a concept.

Despite her improvement, her life was about fear, and it had been forever. At twenty-four, she'd resigned herself to living inside the bubble her father had created for her, going from limo to apartment to business appointments that had all been prescreened and determined safe.

She knew beyond any doubt that anyone looking at her life would believe it was perfect. Why wouldn't they? She had more money than anyone truly should, she'd been given her father's fast metabolism and her mother's striking blue eyes. Her education was exemplary, and if she decided she didn't want to do anything but shop for the rest of her life, she had the means to do just that.

She knew that her agoraphobic tendencies appeared to many as conceit and arrogance. The fact that she was so terrified of being kidnapped that her world had shrunk to a stultifying routine meant nothing. There were real problems out there; she just had an active imagination and a constant state of terror that kept her from enjoying the gifts she'd been given.

She walked outside the building to the busy street,

her gaze fixed on the limo parked just a few feet away. Michael, her driver, opened the back door for her. To those hurrying past he seemed like any other limo driver. Black suit, white shirt, humble demeanor. But behind his dark glasses he was scanning the area with laser intensity and the reason his jacket wasn't buttoned was so that he could, if necessary, get to his weapon in a heartbeat. He drove her, but that was his secondary job.

She passed him closely as she got into the back of the car and marveled again at his face. He wasn't classically handsome. Too many sharp edges and flaws. But his looks had grown on her since he'd come on board six months ago. She hadn't really thought about him that way in the beginning. There were lots of people in her life whose job it was to keep her safe. Some of them were also dear friends—like Elizabeth, her assistant—but most weren't. Her father didn't like her getting too comfortable with the staff, and she'd fallen into the terrible habit of seeing them as employees, not people.

Michael had turned into something else altogether. Not a friend, not really. They never did anything except drive. But they talked. About everything.

She'd learned he liked reading the Russians—Tolstoy, Dostoyevsky, Turgenev. But he also liked the graphic novels of Frank Miller. She liked to tease him about his comic books, but she'd secretly ordered a few Miller novels online, and they were…well, interesting.

He shut the door, then walked around to the driver's side and settled himself inside. She could see his sunglasses in the rearview mirror and wished, as always, that he would take them off.

"Where to?"

"Home."

"No stops?"

"Not today."

He smiled at her, and she settled herself back on the cool leather seat.

She'd also learned that he didn't have a girlfriend. Which was a lot more interesting than his taste in books.

MICHAEL PULLED INTO the mess that was traffic in midtown Manhattan, heading toward Tate's Carnegie Hill penthouse. Something out of the ordinary had happened in the session today. He'd seen that the moment she'd stepped out of the building. He'd wait and see if she wanted to talk or if she would call her friend Sara. He liked it when she spoke to Sara. Tate never hid anything from her closest friend, and for the last few months she hadn't whispered into the phone when she talked. It was her way of telling him about her life without seeming to bare it all.

His gaze shifted from the road to the mirror, where he was met by a pair of cornflower-blue eyes. He knew she was smiling and he smiled back, although he shouldn't. When Tate was this flirtatious it meant that she was running from something unpleasant. He'd been right about her session.

"So how's the doctor doing?"

Tate shifted so all he could see of her was her right temple. "Fine."

"Wonder what she talks about when she sees *her* shrink?"

"Probably about how whacked-out her patients are."

"I don't know. She seems pretty professional to me."

"You met her once. For about five seconds."

He grinned. "Yeah, but she was professional for the whole five seconds."

Her eyes were back in focus. Smiling. "Sometimes she comes up with some weird ideas."

"For example?" A cab slipped in front of him, forcing him to slam on the brakes. Hitting the horn was tempting but futile, not to mention illegal.

"Nothing," she said, her voice softer, flatter.

He didn't push. The call to Sara would clear things up. The whole phone ploy was actually pretty smart. It didn't completely break down the barriers between them, but overhearing her chats gave him tremendous insight, which helped him do his job. Besides, she was pretty funny.

Hell, if he had to work as someone's trained pony, he was glad it was Tate. She might be rich as Croesus, but she didn't act like most of the trust-fund babies he'd met. He'd wondered, often, whether she'd be so nice if she didn't live every moment in fear. Poor kid. He wished that shrink would move it along. Let Tate really live while she was still young.

"Did Elizabeth tell you about tomorrow?"

Michael nodded. "She gave me the schedule for the week."

"Good. Okay, well…."

He glanced in the mirror, but she wasn't looking at him. The phone call should be coming right up.

He saw an opening for the damn boat of a limo and

he took it, daring the Yellow cab next to him to interfere. By the time he'd gone a half block Tate had the slim cell phone to her ear.

"Hey, it's me."

He wished he could hear both sides of the conversation, but at least he was privy to Tate's voice.

"I don't know, Sara. I think Dr. Bay's gone over the edge this time. She gave me this article. It's about this nutcase artist-cum-therapist here in New York. He kidnaps people for money."

Michael's hands gripped the steering wheel as he struggled not to turn the limo around, using a sidewalk café as a new traffic lane, and go right back to Dr. Bay's office.

"You have? When did you hear about this?"

What in hell was Bay thinking? Maybe she'd had one too many Xanax this morning.

"She thinks that maybe if I go through the experience when I know it's safe, I'll finally get past it. Trial by fire, I suppose."

Shit, Tate needed a new psychologist—and she needed one now. He could just imagine what her father would say to this crazy business. William would have a heart attack on the spot, but not before he'd had Dr. Bay's license revoked.

When Michael had signed up for the job, he'd had a lot of questions, like why this young woman needed a level of security that would make the president feel safe. William had told him that kidnapping was a danger and that he would go to any lengths to protect Tate.

Michael had agreed that someone with her wealth

was a target, but guards 24-7? Ex-CIA case officers as a cook and a secretary?

Then he'd heard bits and pieces about the basis for the paranoia. At fifteen, Tate and her cousin had been kidnapped. Tate had escaped out a small bathroom window, but her cousin had been murdered. Tate had done her best to find the kidnapper's hideout, but she'd been so traumatized she hadn't been much help. Then, five years after that, when Tate was in college, there had been another attempt. A couple of local idiots had taken her at gunpoint from her car, demanding two million dollars. Luckily the kidnappers had been inept fools, and the FBI had found them within hours, but the experience had scarred Tate deeply, and her father had become determined that she'd never be vulnerable again. As his fortune had grown, so had his security measures.

"I hyperventilated," Tate said with a self-deprecating laugh. "But seriously, Sara, I promised her I'd give it some thought."

He finally reached Carnegie Hill and turned the limo toward the entrance to her building, easing up on the gas so he wouldn't miss out on the end of the call.

"I can't see it, either," Tate said. "But she asked me something just before I left. She asked what my life would be like if I wasn't afraid. I had no answer for her."

Michael was all for Tate getting over her fear of being kidnapped, but throwing her into the fire was ridiculous. There had to be another way.

"We're here. I'll call you later. We'll talk some more, but don't worry. I'm not saying yes."

He pulled the car into the driveway that would take

them to the underground garage. There was a spot near the elevator that was reserved for the limo, which made things easier. But he'd ride up to Tate's place with her, make sure she got inside safely.

The garage itself was extraordinarily well lit. Not just now but day and night. That was courtesy of William Baxter, who spared no expense in keeping his only daughter safe. Elizabeth would be upstairs doing typical assistant things while maintaining her sharp-shooter status and carrying a concealed but legal 9 mm Glock. Everyone who worked with Tate had a similar skill set: good at the normal stuff that helped Tate get through her days, great at the stuff that would scare the bejesus out of the most hardened criminals, if they only knew.

Hell, right now three men would be observing every inch of the penthouse via the most sophisticated cameras in the world. If Tate so much as tripped, there would be at least three trained security personnel to pick her up within sixty seconds.

He parked the limo, then got out to open the back door. Tate gave him a look before she tucked her purse under her arm and climbed out. It had amazed him when he'd first started this gig that she could maneuver herself out of the backseat with such grace. Then he'd realized she'd been doing it her whole life. This was the kind of car that had taken her to school. To the movies. It wasn't just for prom night or a funeral. It was part and parcel of her daily existence.

She headed toward the elevator and pressed the button. There was another example of how she wasn't like so many other overprivileged women: she pressed her own buttons. She made her own phone calls. She did her best to keep up with the lives of those on her staff, although the ex-agent types tended to be on the private side.

The elevator had one of those shiny doors that could double as a mirror, but he kept his gaze lowered. Tate, who was attractive and always kept herself looking sharp, didn't like being watched. Which was fine. It wasn't his job to look at her. He had to keep her safe, which meant looking at everything that surrounded her. Even this elevator. It was checked first thing every morning for bugs, for explosive devices, for anything that could possibly harm its inhabitants.

There wasn't even a long way up—five floors. Since she owned the whole penthouse, it made security easier up there. All told, there were twelve guys who worked for him, and they rotated duty so that none of them ever got too comfortable. Some of the team had been with Tate for years, but Michael had recruited his four top men. It hadn't taken long for all of them to become a unit he could be proud of.

The elevator door opened, and Tate glanced his way before she stepped into the hallway.

He joined her, checking the small area for anything hinky. She had her key out, and he watched as she unlocked both deadbolts. She had such delicate hands. Long, graceful. Her nails were on the short side and they were polished some creamy color that was just a little darker than her skin. No rings, no jewelry at all except for the small diamond-stud earrings. She wasn't a flashy kind of woman. In fact, she did everything she could to blend in. But there was something she couldn't hide—or change: she was a class act. Everything about her said she had money, background, education. She was different, exceptional. Anyone who passed her in the street would know it.

"Thank you," she said.

"You'll be in for the rest of the night?"

"I will."

"All right, then. I'll wait until I hear the deadbolts click in."

She smiled and her pale cheeks filled with a blush. He knew she wanted to ask him in. That her flirting wasn't just about avoidance. She toyed with the idea of having an affair with him, and it made him feel good that she did. Of course, there was no way it could happen. Even if it wasn't completely unethical and dangerous for him to be with Tate, there was no way. She was American royalty and he was a bodyguard. More than one universe apart.

He took two steps back. That was all she needed to decide that today wasn't the day to be bold. She went inside and closed the door. True to his word, he waited until both locks clicked into place. Then he got out his two-way radio and made sure the man on duty had her safe and sound.

By the time he was halfway down to the garage he'd already decided he was going to find out everything he could about this joker who kidnapped people for money.

# 2

MICHAEL STRAIGHTENED his tie as he waited for Tate to come to the door. They were going to her father's place, which never made for an easy day. William was a powerful man who'd made millions—actually, billions—in construction and real estate. He and his brother Joseph had started small, but they'd been smart and ruthless and they'd gotten some prime government contracts that had taken them from their roots in Missouri to penthouses in half the major cities in the world. Although they'd been more successful than anyone could have imagined, there were costs involved, including a daughter and heir so terrified of being kidnapped that she barely lived a life.

Michael knew there was a real threat and that measures had to be taken, but there was also a need for balance. At least some room for Tate to breathe. Unfortunately there wasn't much an outsider could do. Especially not someone as low on the totem pole as a bodyguard.

He heard the locks slide open one after the other. The door swung open to reveal Tate dressed in a pair of beige pants, a pale yellow silky blouse and enough makeup to tell him that she'd had another crappy night.

"Michael. I'm running later than I should. Come in while I finish gathering my things."

He stepped inside a foyer as large as his apartment. He'd grown accustomed to the world of the rich, although it never ceased to make him wonder who the hell was in command of the planet.

It wasn't easy to like the very rich, either, although Tate was pretty decent. She never actually meant to make people feel like poor slobs. It just happened.

She went toward the kitchen, and Michael took the opportunity to do a surprise inspection. He moved his right hand in a specific signal, one that would easily be missed if his people weren't on the ball, watching his every move on the cameras set discreetly around the penthouse. Two minutes would be all the time he needed. If E.J. wasn't here by then, he'd be looking for a new job.

He made it in one minute and forty-two seconds. E. J. Packer was young, twenty-four, but he'd been an excellent sniper in the Delta Force when he'd been badly scarred in a shoot-out with Syrian terrorists. He hadn't lost any of his ability, but he was distinct now, recognizable for the angry red mess that was the left half of his face. Michael didn't give a shit about that. He wanted a crack team that not only knew what to do at the party but understood that no matter where they worked—or for whom—it was a military operation and there was no excuse, ever, for slacking off.

He nodded at E.J. "That was close."

"I'll do better next time, sir."

"I know you will. Carry on."

E.J.'s shoulders moved just enough to let Michael know he hadn't let go of the trappings of being a soldier.

Didn't matter as long as he did the job. As long as he didn't make Tate feel like a bug under a microscope.

The young man disappeared, melting away as silently as he'd entered. Michael thought about going into the kitchen, talking to Pilar, Tate's personal chef. But he just walked the perimeter of the foyer, checking out the artwork.

This place had always felt more like a museum than a home. Marble floors, antiques of inestimable worth, paintings he recognized because they were masterpieces. He took in a deep breath to combat the tightening of his throat. It wasn't that he resented her for having the money. Okay, so he resented it a little. But what really pissed him off is that this was what his life had come to. Babysitting.

"Michael?"

He turned at Tate's voice.

"Would you like some coffee? I'm going to be another ten minutes or so. I've already warned Father."

"Sure, that'd be great." He waited until Tate disappeared back into the hallway, then he went into the kitchen.

Pilar was there pouring him the promised cup of coffee. He wasn't one for fancy java or any of that flavored crap, but he had to admit the coffee in Tate's kitchen was some of the best he'd ever had. He wasn't sure what it was and he'd never asked. No chance he'd ever get those beans for his coffeemaker.

"How are you, Michael?"

Pilar was born in Brazil and moved to the U.S. when she went to college at eighteen. Her accent made her seem exotic and sophisticated. Or maybe that was just Pilar. She had trained at the CIA—the Culinary Institute of America—which was one of the reasons she was working as Tate's chef, but she'd also trained at the other CIA, and that was why she had a chef's coat with a custom pocket that held her Sig Sauer.

"I'm fine," he said, taking the too-delicate cup from her hand. "How's the new kid working out?"

She smiled at him, and he tried to remember if he'd ever seen her without her deep crimson lipstick expertly applied to her generous mouth.

"Don't you think of anything but business?"

"No."

She laughed. "No wonder you have no love life."

"How do you know?"

"Michael, my dear, if you can resist me, then you can resist anyone."

He held back his own grin. "How do you know I'm not gay? Living the wild life with my lumberjack boyfriend?"

Her laughter actually echoed in the kitchen. It was ridiculously large, like something out of Windsor Castle, all for one woman whose only guests were business associates, all of them involved with the Baxter Foundation, a charitable organization funded by Baxter, run by Tate.

"Believe me, I'd know if you were gay," Pilar said. She picked up her own cup and took a sip, leaving no trace of her lipstick on the rim. "It's a shame you don't let yourself relax, though. It isn't healthy."

"I relax."

"I don't even think you know the definition of the word."

"What word?"

Michael turned to see Tate standing at the hallway door. "Are you ready?"

"Not really, and we're not late. I just got off the phone with a very obstinate woman at the MacArthur Foundation and I need to calm down."

"So you're getting coffee?" he asked as she handed Pilar another cup.

"Yes. I am."

"Okay by me."

She took the full cup back but didn't drink. Instead she focused her attention on him. Her expression became pensive and she opened her mouth, but then a blush stole over her cheeks and she turned to Pilar. Two sips and five quiet minutes later they were in the elevator, on the way down to the limo. Tate looked at her shoes the whole time.

SHE STARED OUT HER tinted window, watching New York pass by, chewing once again on the idea Dr. Bay had fed her last week. It was easy to make excuses for her fears, which were, in fact, legitimate. She could be kidnapped, held for ransom, murdered. Such things had occurred, could occur again. It made sense to be wary, to keep her guard up.

On the other hand, her guard was up so high she couldn't see the world behind it. Yes, it could all go to hell tomorrow. But it hadn't gone to hell yesterday or the day before or many years before that. She'd put all her eggs in the fear basket, and wouldn't she feel like the biggest idiot on earth if she went on to live to a ripe old age, completely safe and having missed the whole thing.

She sighed as she gazed at the back of Michael's head. His dark hair was wavy and thick and she wondered if the messy-chic was on purpose or just truculence. Somehow she doubted Michael owned mousse or gave a damn about how he looked—which, in her opinion, was incredibly juicy even on his bad days. It helped that he kept himself in battle-ready shape. He even walked as if daring anyone to try anything funny.

How had she let her fear of being kidnapped morph into a fear of everything? College had started out so well. She'd finally been able to put Lisa's death behind her, at least enough to get by, and then—whoosh!—it all had vanished on that one awful day when Ian Stark and Bruce Halliday had kidnapped her.

After that everything had gone to hell. Her relationship with Graydon, never great to begin with, had soured until she'd had to get out. She'd started spending more and more time in her apartment, only leaving to go to class or one of her self-defense classes, which, instead of making her feel more in control, had brought her terror into sharper relief.

She had given in to the panic attacks, the nightmares—and they'd taken over. And now look at her. She hadn't even been able to ask Michael a simple question. She saw him almost every day. They talked and talked, and yet when it came to something as foolish, as personal, as the origins of the scar on his chin, she became tongue-tied and shy as a kitten. It wasn't as if she wanted to ask him if he preferred boxers to briefs. The scar was right there for anyone to see.

Pathetic.

HE STOOD AGAINST THE wall in the executive dining room along with the two ex-Secret Service agents who protected William Baxter. One, Jim, was William's driver, and the other, Peter, was his executive secretary. But mostly they were there to make sure no one got too close. Paranoia hadn't hurt just Tate but her father, too.

Michael despised this part of his job. It would be different if he'd been protecting a president or prime minister, someone who was doing something for the good of the people, not just an industrialist's daughter. He'd tried to justify his position, given that Tate ran the Baxter Foundation and that they did help people with their dollars, but that had grown as stale as the sandwich he'd been offered in the staff kitchen.

He shifted his gaze to William. The man was sixty-four but he looked a hell of a lot older. He could afford the best of everything, including plastic surgery for that turkey neck of his, but he preferred to spend his money on things that others would covet. This building, his home, his airplane. His daughter. It was hard for Michael to keep his composure when he was with William and Tate. The man treated her like a child. Like an invalid child. And she let him.

He shifted his position so that he wouldn't get stiff. In all his years in the military he should have grown accustomed to standing, to waiting. He still hated it. He'd rather face a dozen armed men than do nothing but stand and watch.

Tate laughed, which was a damn rare, good thing. He wondered if she knew that she was pretty. That her long neck, her skin, the way her eyes lit up when she

was captivated made her incredibly appealing. He
didn't think she thought of herself that way at all. She
dressed in the camouflage of a woman who doesn't
want to be noticed. Beige, cream, taupe, khaki. Pale
colors that blended with her pale skin.

His thoughts jumped to the information he'd down-
loaded about the kidnap artist. Jerry Brody was his
name. Michael had read everything he'd been able to
find. The guy sounded like a first-class jerk, full of
himself and how he was exploring the "human condition." Michael didn't understand how anyone could be
fooled by his shtick. Yes, he had a degree in psy-
chology, but come on. According to the papers, he'd
kidnapped dozens of people, stolen them from their
homes, their cars, from movie theaters. He'd tied them
up, blindfolded them, taken them to a small, barren
room and kept them isolated. Feeding and communi-
cation were used as weapons to make the experience
more realistic.

That Tate's shrink proposed this idea was unbeliev-
able. Where had William found this quack? The
woman should lose her license over a stunt like this.

Michael had to make sure Tate wasn't going to agree
to it. That was all. If it came down to it, he'd talk to
William. No way the old man would put up with this
crap.

Tate laughed again. It was good to see her so
relaxed, but Jesus. They were at the top of the Baxter
Building in the middle of Manhattan, on the sixtieth
floor, in the executive dining room. Every table but one
was empty. None of the managers or supervisors or
whoever normally used this place were allowed in

when Tate came to lunch. In addition to Michael and the two Secret Service men, there were also men stationed at the door, in the kitchen and at the elevator.

Her whole goddamn life was one big maximum-security prison.

TATE SETTLED AGAINST the black leather seat of her limo, avoiding Michael's gaze as he shut the door. She had to blink away sudden tears, swallow a lump in her throat.

The lunch had been fine. Her father was in good spirits, the food superb, the conversation productive. All had been right with the world...until she'd looked at Michael and caught the pity in his eyes.

It was only then that she'd seen the empty tables all around them, heard the echo of cutlery on china. Shame had hit her with a wicked gut punch, and she hadn't been able to touch her sorbet.

He hadn't said a word to her, not in the elevator nor in the garage. He'd treated her with respect, as always. He'd even given her one of his rare smiles as he'd opened the limo door. But his look of pity lingered in her mind's eye.

Pathetic. There wasn't an area of her life that was free from the effects of her own personal monster. Her father only wanted her to be safe and happy, but she didn't feel, either. She liked administering the trust, but there again she did almost everything from her home office. Her world had shrunk to a pinpoint. If it wasn't for Sara... How had this happened?

"Tate?"

"Yes?"

"Home?"

"Yes, thank you, Michael."

"No shopping to do?"

"Not today, no."

"Okay."

His voice sounded normal. No reprimand in his tone at all. And in that heartbeat she made her decision. She would do it. Be kidnapped. She would call Dr. Bay first thing tomorrow and she'd start the process.

Her hands shook at the enormity of the decision. Which just made her more determined. This was her life, and as of this moment she was taking control.

# 3

MICHAEL SAT AT HIS kitchen table, a cold beer half-finished, newspaper and magazine articles spread in front of him. All of them seemed to cover the same territory about Jerry Brody and his lunacy. Unfortunately none of the articles gave him enough information about Brody's clients to lead him to an actual ID. Michael had put in calls to every one of the reporters, but only two had phoned back, neither one willing to name those who had used Brody's service.

He'd even left a message with Brody himself, his intention to pose as a would-be client, which would give him a lot of information, and he'd also ask for personal referrals.

He just hoped that all this work was for nothing. He didn't imagine Tate would be foolish enough to walk into a nightmare scenario like this, but he had to plan as if it were a go. What he couldn't decide was whether he should tell William about this or just go see Dr. Bay himself.

He stretched his head to the right, then the left, trying to work out some of the tension in his neck and shoulders. What he needed to do was get his ass to the gym. He hadn't been in three days, and that was unacceptable. Besides keeping him in fighting shape, his brutal workouts were his best defense against stress and depression.

He didn't belong in New York, at least not like this. He should be in Iraq or Afghanistan, doing what he'd been trained to do. Not babysitting.

He took another swig of beer. Of all the useless things in his life, wishing he could change his situation was the stupidest. He'd left the military of his own free will—but not because he'd wanted to. He still felt the decision was the right one, even if it did mean he'd have to live this life.

Needing the distraction, he went back to reading the last of the articles about Brody. It was as useless as the rest. He turned the page anyway. Maybe—

A knock at his door made him jump, but he relaxed just as quickly. Only one person came to his apartment these days. One person Michael didn't want to see.

Yep, it was Charlie. The real reason Michael was a glorified babysitter.

His brother knocked again, louder this time.

Michael went back to the table and gathered his work into a file. That he put into the small safe in a cabinet in the living room. Only then did he let his brother in.

"What the hell?" Charlie said as he crossed the living room to the kitchen. "Were you in the crapper?"

"You ever heard of calling first?"

Charlie opened the fridge and took one of Michael's Heinekens. He looked like shit, but that wasn't unusual. Charlie was the only member of his family still living, and that was some kind of miracle because the way he played so fast and loose with drugs, booze and the horses, he should have been dead years ago. Nothing worked in Charlie's life, never had. Ever since Michael could remember, Charlie had been the screw-up. Part of that was probably due to their mother's death when Charlie was only five, but that excuse could only go so far.

Their old man had tried his best to get Charlie some help, but there wasn't a rehab center on the East Coast Charlie hadn't ditched.

Michael supposed he loved his brother on some level, but that level was buried beneath a steaming pile of resentment. The old man had made him swear to take care of Charlie. Michael didn't have the guts to go against a deathbed wish, although it probably would have been better for both of them.

Michael would still be in military intelligence, and Charlie…

"Mikey, listen. I know I promised I wouldn't ask for no more money, but I'm in a hell of a spot."

Michael fetched his own beer and sat down in his leather club chair. He might as well be comfortable for the argument that was about to start the moment he said, "I told you, Charlie, the bank of Michael is closed."

Charlie sat down on the couch, his beefy hand holding on to his beer so tightly Michael wouldn't have been surprised if it shattered. He really did look like shit. He'd been about thirty pounds overweight for years now, but at least when he was younger he'd been solid. Now there was a look of undercooked dough about him. It didn't help that he was wearing a filthy

T-shirt and jeans that hadn't seen the inside of a washing machine in God knows how long.

"Mikey, you don't understand. I'm in a real mess. I had me this sure thing. You remember that trainer I told you about? The guy with the limp and the broken tooth? He swore, Mikey, swore to God himself that the race was fixed, that he'd done the fixing himself."

"I'm not bailing you out again. We already discussed that. You gave me your word."

"And I meant it. If I hadn't heard the words from that trainer guy for myself, I never would have—"

"Charlie, stop it. I don't care why."

His brother, two years his junior and as different from Michael as day was from night, gave him a look of such hatred it made him sick to his stomach. He'd bailed Charlie out too many times to count, and this was what he got? One no, and Charlie looked as if he could kill him as soon as pass him the salt.

"It's Ed Martini, Mike. You know his reputation. He's gonna kill me."

"He isn't. What good are you gonna do him dead?"

Charlie shook his head, a drop of sweat flying off the end of his long, dirty hair. "He said he was gonna make an example of me. You know what that means? He's gonna kill me, but he's gonna hurt me—bad— before it's over. That dude, Jazz, who works for him? I swear to God, he's a psycho. He loves to hurt people, Mikey. I swear to God."

Michael figured about ten percent of whatever Charlie said was true. The problem was, which part? "I'll pay for you to go back to rehab. And if you stick it out, I'll help you get a job and a place to stay after."

Charlie got up so fast his beer shot out of the bottle, soaking Michael's shirt. "I'm not gonna live long enough to go to goddamn rehab. Don't you listen? They're gonna kill me!"

Michael swore under his breath as he got up. "Just shut up, Charlie. Sit down and shut up. I gotta go change my shirt."

Charlie seemed surprised, as if he hadn't noticed what he'd done, but at least he sat.

Michael went into his bedroom and got another shirt from the dresser. As he changed, he debated giving Charlie the money. It wasn't as if he was rolling in it, but he could spare some. He shouldn't. He'd told his brother in no uncertain terms that he was finished. Yet how could he live with himself if Martini really did kill him?

He tossed the wet shirt in the bathroom hamper, then went back to the living room. Only Charlie wasn't there.

Michael went to the door and looked down the hallway. Charlie was already on the stairs; Michael heard the heavy clump of his brother's boots.

He shut the door, locked the deadbolts and debated getting another beer. It was after ten, though, and he wanted to get up at five to make it to the gym.

In his tiny living room he wiped the trail of beer off the floor, then turned out the lights. He'd more than likely get a call from Charlie tomorrow. And if he was lucky, he'd hear from Jerry Brody, too.

"IF YOU DON'T WANT to do this, we'll stop right here."

Tate tried to squeeze her hands into submission, but the shaking wouldn't stop. "No, I want to. I just…"

"I understand. But remember, you'll have your safe word. You can use it anytime, and the moment you say it, everything stops and you're returned safely to your home. No exceptions."

"So they won't cover my mouth."

"Absolutely not."

Tate believed Dr. Bay and didn't believe her at the same time. Jerry Brody sat across from her at the conference table, while Dr. Bay sat next to her. He didn't look like a performance artist or a therapist. He reminded her, in fact, of the doorman at Sara's apartment building. Round in the middle, shallow in the chest, his balding head his most striking feature.

They'd been in the meeting for half an hour, and Brody had explained that he wasn't in the business of hurting people. He would accommodate Tate's wishes to the best of his ability and he would oversee her adventure himself.

The first time he'd called it an adventure, she'd given him a look that should have seared off his eyebrows. After that, he'd approached her more carefully. Still, she wasn't sure he understood the depth of her phobia.

"I'd like to add that to the contract, Mr. Brody," Dr. Bay said. "No covering of her mouth at any time."

Brody nodded. "That's fine. You realize she won't know when we're going to take her? It's a natural reaction to scream or call out. I don't want any of my people being arrested."

"Please don't talk about me as if I'm not here," Tate said. "As for being arrested, it won't happen if you do your planning adequately. Which reminds me—

we'll have to make sure that Michael knows the plan. If you surprise him, he'll do a lot more than arrest you."

"Michael?"

"Her driver and bodyguard." Dr. Bay put her hand on Tate's. "Don't worry. If we decide to go ahead, we'll bring him into the loop."

"He's not going to like it."

"I don't doubt it."

"Maybe there's a way we can send him on vacation or something," Tate said. She could feel her cheeks fill with the heat of embarrassment, which was something of a surprise. It occurred to her that she didn't want Michael in the loop or to even know this fake kidnapping was being discussed. She knew he'd have serious objections, but worse than that, he'd think she was a fool.

But he wasn't afraid of his own shadow.

"I'm sure," Dr. Bay said, "that once he realizes you'll be completely safe, he won't have any objections. Perhaps he can take a meeting with you, Mr. Brody, and you two can go over his concerns."

Brody might be a self-proclaimed artistic genius, but he wasn't much of an actor. He clearly wanted his show to be run his way, with no interference.

"Let's continue," Tate said. "I'll decide about Michael later."

Dr. Bay smiled. "That's a good idea." She turned to Brody. "Let's discuss constraints."

"I typically use rope and handcuffs. Since she—" He stopped, turned his head a half inch so he was looking at Tate. "Since you'll only be with us for a few hours, the constraints won't be too extreme. And I'll be there every step of the way to make sure nothing goes wrong."

"It won't do me any good to have you go so easy I don't get any part of the experience. I believe the purpose is to make sure I survive, right?"

"I don't think that will be a problem," Dr. Bay said. "You'll feel as if it's real."

Tate blushed again. She got the message loud and clear: her phobia was so severe Brody wouldn't have to do much in the way of convincing her. "Fine. Let's move on."

"YOU'RE INSANE."

"Thank you," Tate said as she handed Sara her plate. Pilar had made a sinful lasagna, which happened to be Tate's favorite dish, but the casserole was large enough to feed an army.

"I'm serious. Personally I think your precious Dr. Bay has a screw loose. This has to be one of the dumbest things I can think of."

Tate took her own plate, which had a small square of lasagna and a spinach salad, and her glass of wine and followed Sara as she made her way up to the solarium on the roof. It was their favorite place to eat, to talk. In her little area of New York the buildings weren't skyscrapers; the view was of Central Park, and her rooftop garden was the highest thing around.

Sara got herself comfy, and Tate thought her friend had never looked better. Sara had been her downstairs neighbor since second grade, when they'd both lived in a brownstone on East Forty-fourth Street. They'd stayed close all these years.

She had always thought of herself as chubby, even though Tate had told her that size ten wasn't in the least fat and that she was beautiful. It was the company she kept that made her feel big. Sara worked as an editor for *Vanity Fair* magazine, and most of the women she knew were bulimic and looked as if they'd been starved.

This year, though, something had changed. Sara had finally decided that she'd just focus on being healthy—tonight's lasagna notwithstanding—and she'd been working out with a private trainer for months.

"You look fabulous."

Sara had just put a large forkful of pasta in her mouth, and at Tate's compliment she nearly choked. When she finally got her breath back, she shook her head. "No way you're changing the subject."

"I wasn't trying to change anything. I just think you look—"

"Fabulous. Right. Now here's my question—have you or haven't you invited Michael inside after work?"

Tate felt the instant rise of heat in her cheeks. "Not yet."

"Not yet." Sara put her fork down and somehow managed to look stern and motherly despite the fact that she was Tate's age and her hair was a mass of wild blond curls. "You can't even ask Hotty McSwoon into your home, let alone into your bed, and you're going to get kidnapped? By strangers? With rope and handcuffs? You don't see a problem with this?"

"I know. It sounds crazy. But the whole reason I haven't invited Michael in is because I'm scared. Of everything. Or haven't you noticed?"

"Of course I know you're scared, but let's look at the progression here. First kidnap, then sex?"

"Yes. And I don't know that he'd even want to have sex."

Sara laughed. "Oh, please. The way you two look at each other in that limo? I'm surprised you both don't come at every stoplight."

"Sara!"

"It's true and you know it."

Tate got busy with her lasagna, wishing now she'd taken a much bigger piece. Just thinking about Michael was enough to get her all hot and bothered, and even though Sara was her closest friend, she didn't like to feel like this except in the privacy of her own bedroom.

"Tate, what's going on in that head of yours?"

"Nothing."

"Talk to me, girl. This is a huge decision."

"I know. I'm just so tired of being me. If I could have an exorcism, I would. But I don't think it's a devil that makes me so scared. I've set up my whole life to be safe, but the cost is huge. I would love to go to the gym with you. I'd love to go back to Italy. I can travel anywhere in the world, but all I see is this place." She felt tears burn her eyes, and dammit, she didn't want to cry. "I really think this kidnapping thing will change me. I have to take the chance."

"What does Michael think?"

"He agrees with you. That it's insane. But I have to go with my gut on this. I've made sure that I can stop things in a minute if I need to. I hope I don't have to. I want to be a real person, not a shadow." She pushed her plate away, suddenly not hungry. "I need you to support me, Sara. Please. I need all the good karma I can get."

Sara reached over and put her hand on Tate's. "I'll support you no matter what, okay? Think it through. Make sure this isn't going to make things worse."

"It can't get much worse."

Sara sighed. She looked around the solarium, at all the plants and flowers, the miniature fruit trees and the tall grasses by the fountain. "I want you to be happy. For what it's worth, I think Michael's a really great guy, and you could do a lot worse than getting back in the game with him. But let him in on the kidnap plan. Let him make sure nothing goes haywire."

"No. He can't be there or it won't be real."

"It's not going to be real."

"You know what I mean."

Sara sighed. "Yeah, I do."

Tate grinned. "Can you stick around for a movie?"

"Sure I can. But only if I get to pick."

"We're not going to watch *Notting Hill* again."

"Spoilsport."

"Deal with it."

Sara lifted her glass of wine. "To stubborn women."

Tate raised her own glass. "Amen."

SHE DIDN'T THINK about the kidnapping or Michael until after Sara left. Tate had gone to her bedroom where she'd washed and gotten into her sleep shirt, then climbed into her bed. She wished she had a cat or a puppy, something to sleep with her. Her father was terribly allergic, so she'd never had her own pet, but this was her house, and if he didn't like it, he didn't have to visit.

The moment she closed her eyes she knew it wasn't a pet she wanted sharing her bed. She wanted Michael.

He really was an exceptional man. She knew he wasn't thrilled with his life, that he wished he was back doing his 007 thing, but when they were together, him in the front seat, her in the back, there was a connection between them. Even Sara had noticed.

Of course, there was no real future with Michael, but that was all right. Sara had hit the nail on the head—Michael would be ideal as her first after so, so long. He'd be gentle and caring....

A fling. That's all she wanted. Really.

# 4

AS HE STOOD LEANING against the limo, waiting for Tate to finish her shopping, Michael thought once more about going to William. It had been a week since Tate had told him she'd agreed to the kidnapping. In that time Michael had met with Brody, talked with three of his past "victims" and gone over the plan about fifty times. He still thought it was a ridiculous and dangerous game, but Tate had made up her mind.

There was still time to go to William, who would put a stop to this nonsense, but Tate was adamant that her father be kept out of the loop. When he'd suggested that he come along for the stunt, Tate had nearly wept insisting that he stay the hell away.

Wasn't going to happen, of course. Although Brody had said he'd give no warning before the actual snatch, Michael was going to see him tomorrow to persuade him that it was in Brody's best interest to take him along. Tate wouldn't know, and that was fine, but there was no way he was going to let her get taken to some unknown location for an indeterminate period of time without him watching every goddamn second. He could just see himself trying to explain to William how Tate had been hurt—or worse—while he'd been watching basketball on ESPN.

Of course, if Brody continued to object, Michael had a plan B. He always had a plan B.

He checked his watch and figured he'd give Tate another five minutes. She was in the Prada store having a fitting. He still couldn't figure that damn store out. There was practically nothing on display. It was all hidden in some way that clearly appealed to women.

He'd waited out enough fittings to know he couldn't rush her, but he also didn't like her to be out of his sight. Of course, Elizabeth was with her, and he trusted her. Even better, Tate trusted her. A former CIA case officer, Elizabeth knew her way around a weapon.

His cell phone rang. It was George, one of his tech guys who worked on the alarm system at Tate's. They were replacing some of the equipment, and Michael had asked for regular updates. As in all things concerning Tate, he wanted the hard-core work to be done when she was sleeping or out of the penthouse. She tended to get nervous when she caught glimpses of what it really took to keep her safe.

"What's going on?"

"It's all good, boss. We have the equipment in and we've just finished the test run. We'll be all cleaned up in ten."

"What did you think of the test?"

"It's everything they promised."

"Good, I—" He saw Tate come out of the shop carrying two large bags. Just as she reached the center of the sidewalk, she stopped and handed the bags to

Elizabeth, then she looked inside her purse. "George, she's coming. I'll talk—"

A movement caught his attention, someone in a hooded coat right behind her. A second later the man shoved Elizabeth into a passing group of students. Michael tossed the phone and got out his weapon as he ran. A white van drove up onto the sidewalk, the side door wide-open. The hooded man shoved Tate inside and the van took off.

He lifted his weapon to shoot out a tire, but civilians crowded in front of him and he lost the shot. Brody had covered the license plate with mud, and there was nothing else identifying about the van as it turned the corner out of his view.

He raced back to the limo, cursing Dr. Bay fifty ways to Sunday. If it was the last thing he did, he was going to find Jerry Brody and break his neck.

He picked up the cell phone he'd dropped. It still worked, and as he pulled out of the shopping mall valet parking lot, he hit *2.

"Elizabeth here."

"I'm going after her," he said, "but I'm dropping off the limo and taking my own vehicle. Got that?"

"Yes, sir. I'm sorry—"

"Just make sure Daddy doesn't get inquisitive. If all goes well, I'll have her back by nightfall."

"Yes, sir."

He clicked off the phone, tossed it on the seat and pulled out another electronic device, the one the size and shape of a BlackBerry. It was actually a GPS—a global positioning system—with only one target. The moment he saw the light on the map he relaxed. He'd find her and bring her home. There would be plenty of time to kill Brody afterward.

For now, he concentrated on not killing any pedestrians or getting arrested as he broke a great many laws. He had to get out of this limo if he wanted to have the least bit of stealth. He'd taken his motorcycle to work this morning, which was a good thing. He could move quickly and get into tight spots with that baby, and there weren't many cars on the road that could catch him.

Michael figured the van was registered to Brody and that it was heading toward Long Island, where Brody lived. But he wasn't a hundred percent sure and he wasn't going to take any chances.

Tate knew about the GPS tracker—at least the one in her wristwatch. She didn't know about the one in her purse. But that was fine. She didn't need to know everything. Besides, if she hadn't actually passed out from fear, she'd be too busy with her panic attacks to think about global positioning systems.

SHE WAS IN A VAN and there was a bag over her head. Tate could barely feel her hands or her feet, but she could feel the bag being sucked into her mouth as she struggled for breath. The air was foul, sick, and her heart pounded hard in her chest.

"Stop," she said, only it was a croak, not really a word. "Stop." It was only a tiny bit better. They wouldn't hear her. He'd promised to stop if she asked him to, but he had to hear her.

"Stop!"

That was louder, that was more of a scream, but the

van kept going, kept rocking, and no one touched her or listened. She tried to kick out, to make them listen, but her legs were tied together and she could hardly move.

"Stop! Stop!" She used all her strength to thrash, to get their attention. And her heart—it was filling her chest and squeezing her lungs so she couldn't breathe.

"Stop, stop, stop, stop!"

No one answered. She was alone and she was going to die in the back of this van. There was no air, no escape. It was over and there was so much she hadn't done.

The blackness came from the inside out. It was welcome.

HE MADE IT TO THE garage in Tate's building, then jumped out of the vehicle and climbed onto his rebuilt Suzuki GSX. He docked his GPS just above the speedometer and squealed out of the garage, heading toward Long Island. He wasn't exactly sure where Brody lived, but he thought it might be Little Neck.

Didn't matter. He was following the purse. Brody had no reason to scan Tate for a GPS, so he had no need to get rid of her purse. Even if the pervert wanted to take her clothes, they'd still be in the van.

Trouble was, it was Friday and it was four-thirty, and the expressway was a parking lot. He could get around the cars all right, but there was a great chance he could be popped in the process. The last thing he needed now was to have to explain this to the highway patrol.

He inched the bike forward and thought again about Brody. The man wasn't exactly living on his performance art, despite charging an arm and a leg for his kidnappings. Michael knew Tate had already given him ten grand—half the fee. But Brody himself lived off his wife's income. She was some big cosmetic surgeon who Botoxed politicos and movie stars. She was why he could afford to play with his art.

As he put his leg down once again to wait for traffic to move, he watched the blip on the GPS moving steadily forward on the same expressway, only about ten miles ahead.

Screw it. He'd explain to the police if he had to. In the meantime, he was gonna find Tate.

Swerving the bike into the fire lane, he gunned it. He tried to keep an eye out for cops, but between looking at the signal and trying not to be killed by motorists, he had his hands full.

There was a car stuck in his way a few miles in, so he went back into traffic. Despite the laws against it in New York, he did the bob and weave, skating past SUVs and Toyotas with a couple of inches to spare.

He couldn't understand how the van was making such good time, but as the minutes ticked by and the GPS kept purring, he closed the distance.

Just as he thought he might get a visual, he heard the dreaded sound of a police siren.

Glancing back, he saw the NYHP coming up the fire lane.

Michael slowed down and found himself a nice place to idle right in front of a grocery truck. Traffic moved at about five miles an hour, and he just stayed put, preparing his explanation.

The blip on the GPS went farther away with each painstaking inch, and so did the siren. Finally he saw the lights in his side mirror. Even the cops weren't going very fast. When they reached his side, they didn't stop, and he let out a held breath. They were after something else, an accident probably, but with them so close he didn't dare pull any stunts.

He tried to be patient. He wasn't successful.

TATE WOKE, STILL IN the darkness of the rocking vehicle. She had no moisture at all in her throat and she felt as if she would choke to death. She tried to cry out again, to tell them they had it wrong, but she couldn't.

Her tears felt hot on her cheeks as her heart pumped beyond its endurance. She thought of her father, how furious he would be at her for getting herself into this mess. How he would have to live with the fact that her death was her own fault.

She thought of Michael and how all this could have been prevented if she hadn't been so vain. He would have stopped this, he would have saved her.

She'd wasted so much of her life, only to end up throwing her life away on a stunt. On this idiotic game.

What she didn't understand is why they weren't following the agreement. Brody had signed the contract. Didn't he realize he'd be in trouble once they discovered he'd ignored the rules?

She gasped again, licked a tear off her lip. She would give anything, any amount of money, if only they would let her go. She'd never do anything this stupid again. She'd be good, she'd pray every night, she'd—

The truck turned, causing her to roll to her right,

then stabilize again. Maybe they were close to wherever they were taking her. They'd have to listen then, wouldn't they?

But she probably wasn't going to make it. Not when she couldn't catch her breath. Not when her chest was about to explode. It was over. Her life was ending. What a pathetic waste.

IT HAD BEEN AN accident, a big one. Two SUVs, one overturned, a fire truck, an ambulance and several patrol cars. Michael had no choice but to wait until he'd passed the worst of it before he could even get to a decent speed.

The van was already past it all. It had turned off the expressway onto the surface streets of Port Washington. He knew the area, but not well.

By the time he got to the right exit he saw the van heading toward Sands Point. According to Michael's research, neither Brody nor the wife were Sands Point rich. Hell, he knew of one estate that was for sale there right now—price tag of twenty-eight million. That was William Baxter territory, and it didn't sit right.

The traffic wasn't all that great even now that he was off the LIE. Too many commuters coming in from the city, trying to make it to their nice Long Island homes. The blip on the GPS had stalled. He lifted the unit from the cradle and pressed a couple of buttons. Seacoast Lane. That was on the very edge of Sands Point.

He'd driven Tate to Sands Point once about four months ago, to a literary luncheon given by an author who lived there. Susan somebody. Tate and he had talked about the village. She'd told him that there were no stores of any kind in Sands Point. Only homes and gardens and an animal shelter. The residents—who included the CEO of a large pharmaceutical company, a former governor of New York and the family that owned the estate that many believe was the inspiration for "East Egg" in Fitzgerald's *Gatsby*—were all rich enough that they could live in this garden suburb where the gates and the security guards kept out all but the anointed.

None of that colorful history helped him now. He drove past well-tended yards and kids toting back-packs filled to the limit. Even the frequent suburban stops didn't slow him down as much as the express-way traffic, and soon he was in Port Washington, the town that supported the wealthy lives of those who lived in Sands Point.

It was all so peaceful out here. No honking horns, hardly any pedestrians on the main street. Only twenty-five miles from Manhattan, it felt like another world.

As he approached the gated community, Michael turned his attention to his GPS screen. The blip had stayed right there at Seacoast. He pressed another button, moving in on the target.

Not a second later he was looking at an aerial view of 200 Seacoast. It was a huge estate with only one big semicircular road in and out. The house looked large enough to supply a battalion, and the grounds were ex-pansive. It had to be at least twenty acres. The estate was also surrounded on three sides by Long Island Sound.

Michael put all his concentration now on getting to

Seacoast. First he had to get past the guards, but that was ridiculously simple. He followed another motorcycle—one with a teenager driving—gave the guard a wave and that was that. Then he found the estate, and it was just as impressive as the GPS had indicated.

Ditching his bike was simple in the vast acres of old trees. The last thing he wanted was for Brody to get wind of this rescue and pull some other stupid stunt. By the time he was finished, no one would find his bike.

He had his gun just in case he needed to get pushy. And he had his GPS, but now he used his old-school skills to lead him to his target. He had no idea what kind of security there was and he didn't relish setting off any alarms.

It was still light out, this being the middle of March, so he'd have to be damn careful. He hoped Tate was holding up all right. He also didn't think Sands Point had a psychiatric hospital.

TATE WOKE TO DARKNESS. She lay on a mattress, her right handcuffed to something behind and above her head. Every part of her body ached as she shifted her position.

She tried to think. She'd been in the store with Elizabeth. Karen had been doing a hem. And she'd bought two shirts for her father. It was blank after that.

This was it, of course. The kidnapping. She could feel the familiar symptoms of a panic attack coming over her like a wave. Her accelerated heartbeat, her constricted throat, the narrowing of her vision as she felt as if she was going to die.

"Please," she said, but her voice broke and turned into a sob. "Please, stop this."

She wept and struggled for breath as her stomach churned. It felt as if she was on the water, rolling with the waves, but that couldn't be.

All she wanted was to go home. She'd been crazy to think this was a good idea. It was her worst nightmare come to life. "Please," she said again, this time louder, but no one answered.

He hadn't covered her eyes though he'd said he was going to use a blindfold. But it didn't matter because she couldn't see anything but dark and she couldn't hear anything but her own silent scream. Her body spasmed and she barely felt the pain in her wrist. Everything was too closed, too tight, and she couldn't breathe. If she could just get outside, stop this pounding in her chest…. She would die, and then Michael would never know. He would only remember her being so stupid. *God, please, make it stop. Please, please. Can't breathe.* She was going to throw up, she knew it. She would die like this, in this small room, and she hadn't lived at all.

A light burned her eyes and she struggled more, desperate to get out, get free. Someone was over her, touching her, holding her shoulders.

"Please stop it. Stop. I don't want this. I have to get out, please!"

"Quiet, you damn fool. You're bleeding."

She opened her eyes, adjusted painfully to the light. The man was dark and small and she didn't know him. She'd never seen him before. It wasn't Brody. Brody had promised….

"Stop struggling. You're tearing open your wrist."

But she couldn't. The more he pressed on her shoulders, the more desperate she became. The smell of liquor made her gag, and he stepped back. She opened her mouth, ready to plead, to beg, but she screamed and screamed.

He slapped her hard across the face, and it was as if she'd been doused with cold water. She stopped screaming and for a moment, a horribly vivid moment, she was clear, she was there, in this strange room with the awful man.

"Shut the hell up. You're gonna piss him off—and you don't want to do that."

"Let me go," she whispered, barely recognizing her own voice. "Stop this now. I'll pay you. You won't lose any money, but please let me go."

"You'll pay, all right, but there's no way we're letting you go."

"Where's Brody?"

"Who the fuck's Brody? Just shut up. Be still and it'll be better for you."

"What?"

"If you calm down, I'll put something on your wrist."

"Who are you?"

He smiled, and his teeth were large and his eyes were small. "Don't matter who I am. What matters is who you are."

"You're not Brody."

He shook his head. "You want to bleed to death, that's okay with me, only he don't want his bed all filled with blood, see?"

"Who is he? Where am I?"

"Listen to me. Just give me your father's phone number, okay? That's all you have to do. Then everything'll be just fine."

"What?"

"The phone number. There's nothing else you need to worry about. Just give us the number."

"Why?"

"Look, just give it up. You're a pretty lady. You don't want to get hurt now, do ya?"

"Oh, my God. You're not Brody. This isn't the plan. You've kidnapped me. You're going to kill me."

"Now who said anything about killing you? We just need the number."

She'd awakened from her nightmare straight into hell. This was the real thing. She'd been kidnapped. Every bad dream she'd ever had was true and right now, and there was no bargaining, no going to a safe place. She would die and all she could think as she closed her eyes was that she hoped it wouldn't hurt too badly.

She'd never even asked Michael into her home. And now she'd never get the chance.

# 5

No LIGHTS WERE ON inside the house. From where Michael was hiding, behind a band of large elm trees, it appeared that no one was home and that the exterior lights were all connected to a security system.

Getting to the back of the estate was going to be tricky. The last thing he wanted was a police cruiser catching him trespassing. He supposed he could tell the truth—that he was trying to prevent a fake kidnapping—but he doubted the officers would let him continue on his way.

If it had been his place, he knew just where he'd focus his motion sensors and where he'd put the cameras. There was a very narrow window between this estate and the next where motion sensors became a pain in the ass. It wasn't wide enough for an automobile, but it would work for him as long as the fence held out. There was only one way to find out.

He took off, wondering who owned this place. Now that he was here, he couldn't picture Brody living here. The house was ornate, ostentatious. It spoke of old money with its sculptured gardens and heavy drapes behind the closed windows. Brody was modern and eclectic and he would always want to be seen as avant-garde. Unless this was somehow his wife's estate? That didn't fit, either.

He made his way back far enough that he could hear the ocean. The salty scent had been in the air for a while, but the sound of water lapping against a pier or a dock or a boat… He'd been in enough oceans to have some discernment, but he'd never been a SEAL.

Would he have taken her to a boat? Was that all part of his plan? If so, it was goddamn stupid. A woman with a panic disorder and the ocean didn't mix. It was far too easy to picture an ugly death in a boat.

But perhaps there was some other building behind the main house where he had her. He hoped so. It had been too long since she'd been taken. He doubted Tate was handling things well.

Shit, by now her disappearance had to have made a stir. She was Tate Baxter, after all, and the kidnapping had taken place in broad daylight in a very expensive section of Manhattan. William would be going insane and he would want his security chief's head on a platter.

Well, it had been an interesting job while it'd lasted. Once he got Tate back home, he'd resign and he'd distance himself as much as possible from his team. They didn't need to collect unemployment just because he'd been suckered.

The edge of the main house came into view, and behind it he could see the ocean. There was a yacht, at least a 65 footer, moored at the edge of a small pier. Parked right by the dock was a white van with muddy plates. Lights glowed from inside the yacht, and as he ran faster, he could see a man's silhouette.

There was no other building. They had her on the water. But not for long.

"WAKE UP."

Tate fought to stay cool, but the sharp pains in her wrist and on her arms were more insistent than the man. She opened her eyes. There were more lights on, and she could now see him clearly.

He was of some mixed heritage, maybe black, maybe Hispanic. His eyes were almost golden, which didn't make much sense. He looked intent and excited; he was smiling as he shook her, and his teeth were crooked, large. He exhaled garlic in her face, and she tried to move her head, which hurt worse than her wrist.

"She's awake."

Another voice, a man, older, behind him. She didn't want to see him, but she looked anyway. He was nothing like his companion. She was right about his age. He was tan, and while his hair was completely white, his face was unlined except around his eyes. He seemed very tall, although from her position on the bed that could be an illusion. He wore a blue shirt and he had a large silver chain around his neck.

"Who are you?"

"You don't need to know that," he said. "Move back, Jazz."

The small man let her go and got off the bed. Now she could see the tall man more clearly, and he reminded her of the men in her father's club, pampered and false, as if they'd used every trick in the book to stay the hand of time.

"What's your father's phone number, Tate?"

"I won't tell you."

"Yes, you will. The only question is how much Jazz will hurt you until you do."

The panic started again and she felt a scream building in her throat.

"Just tell us. It will be so much easier."

"You'll kill me if I tell you."

"I'll kill you if you don't."

"Go ahead."

"Oh, no. That's not how we play the game." He nodded at Jazz.

The small man smiled wider, his glee apparent at the anticipation of her pain. He reached over her head and took her hand in his. He pulled it, hard, and the scream grew as it felt as if he were tearing her wrist apart.

She kicked and found that her legs were no long tied together. It didn't matter, though. She couldn't reach anything or stop the tearing. All she could do was scream and thrash, her free arm as useless as her legs.

"Give us the number, Tate. This is only the beginning. He'd like nothing more than to ruin that hand of yours forever. He'll cut it through the artery. He will. Then he'll have to stop the bleeding, and the only way he knows to do that is to cauterize it. You know what that is, don't you?"

The image of her flesh burning made her gag, but there was nothing in her stomach. Maybe she should tell them. Then they'd kill her and it would be over. That was better, wasn't it?

The big man sighed loudly. "Again," he said as if he were asking Jazz to change the channel.

Tate closed her eyes as Jazz reached for her hand. The pain took her breath and, with it, her strength. She knew what they wanted from her father, and just like all those years ago, they would win.

"All right," she said, her voice nothing more than a whisper. "Stop. Please."

Jazz let her go, but it didn't help much. The pain shot up her arm and wrapped around her chest. Was it really just today that she'd been picking out shirts at Prada? That she had daydreamed about Michael looking at her with pride?

"Well?"

She wiped the tears from her cheeks with her free hand, wishing for a miracle, knowing none would come. "212…"

MICHAEL MADE IT TO the pier without the police showing up. Nothing mattered now but getting to Tate. It was too easy to imagine her in serious trouble, the kind that didn't clear up with a cup of tea and a good night's sleep.

His gun in his hand, he moved toward the yacht, the *Pretty Kitty,* and tried not to make any noise. If the yacht owner was at all security-conscious, Michael had already set off the alarm. Nothing he could do about that except prepare. He had to remember to ask questions first, which wasn't his usual MO.

Brody might be an ass, but that wasn't against the law in New York. If Michael killed him, it would be bad. On the other hand, if Brody tried anything stupid, a bullet in the kneecap might just show him the error of his ways.

He made it to the stern, jumped over the gunwale and got a peek at the main saloon. It was just as luxurious as he'd supposed, nicer than his apartment. Up three stairs was the wheelhouse, but there was no one there, either. Everyone, it seemed, was behind doors.

He kept moving alongside the boat, keeping as low a profile as possible. There was a porthole just ahead, slightly higher than his crouch. Making sure he kept quieter than the water, he made his way there and looked inside.

Tate wasn't there. Neither was Brody. But he did know the man sitting at the small table, his beefy hand holding on to a beer bottle.

Charlie.

It didn't compute. What the hell was his brother doing on a boat in Sands Point?

Michael stood, not caring at the moment if Charlie saw him. Unfortunately he didn't hear the footsteps on the dock until one second before the butt of the gun smashed into his temple.

WHEN TATE WOKE, HER first thought was that death hurt like a son of a bitch, and that filled her with such anger she cried out. Only then did it occur to her that she hadn't been killed. That her pain meant that she'd passed out again.

Her heart sank as she realized the ordeal wasn't over. That they were waiting to kill her when she was fully conscious and able to experience everything as it happened.

Didn't they get it? She'd given them her father's phone number, and by now he probably knew she'd been kidnapped and was already gathering up the cash he'd need for her ransom. She wondered how much they were asking, but it really didn't matter. Her father would give them his last cent if he thought he could save her.

But he knew, just as she did, that paying the ransom meant nothing. She would never get off this boat alive. It made perfect sense, now that she thought about it, for them to bring her to a boat. All they had to do was weight her down and toss her overboard. She'd never be found.

She shifted on the bed. Not only was the pain in her wrist getting scary but most of her arm was numb. She was thirsty, too. Normally she drank eight glasses of water a day, but today—was it still Friday?—she hadn't. Which was probably good, because it didn't look as though they were going to give her a bathroom break anytime soon.

She used her free hand to pull the small pillow farther down, which seemed to help the pressure on her wrist. Oddly her heart wasn't beating terribly fast, and she was breathing mostly in the normal range. Even her thoughts were coherent. So, what, now that she was certain she was going to die, the panic was gone?

That made her angrier still. What was this all about? She'd been paralyzed by panic for most of her life and *now* she got all Zen about death? Oh, come on.

She wished she could have one more talk with Dr. Bay. First she'd tell her that her kidnapping idea? Not so bright. That her friend Jerry Brody had played them all for the fools they were. Except for Michael.

Michael hadn't liked this from the start. He was the only one who'd told her she was in danger. Of course, he always thought she was in danger. That was simply how he saw it.

But he didn't only see evil. There was a part of him that yearned for peace—that much she knew for sure. The books he loved, the music he listened to…they were all filled with hope. Yes, even some of the Russians made a case for love and kindness.

She remembered the time he'd told her his favorite piece of music. She'd had to weasel it out of him, and it was the only time she'd ever seen him blush. At first he'd insisted that it was "Highway to Hell." But she'd wheedled him into his true confession. His favorite song was "Clair de Lune" by Debussy. It was one of her favorites, too, but when she'd asked him why he was embarrassed, he'd said it was girlie music. That had really made her laugh. Girlie music.

How was it possible she was smiling? On the verge of death, and still the thought of Michael made her smile.

Of course, the real Michael, the 24-7 Michael, probably wasn't close to the man she'd created in her head. Her Michael was, she had to admit, too perfect. The real Michael would never have met her expectations. He couldn't have. So it was probably good for her to die now, before she'd gotten brave enough to pursue him. Before the disillusionment. Right?

She wiped her eyes, then her wet hand on the bedspread. It wouldn't have hurt her feelings if they could have slept together. Just once. He would have still been her dream man, but she'd have had one night of experiencing his body for real. God, how many nights had she gone to sleep imagining what it would be like with him? How it would have felt to have Michael fill her, take her. More than that, kiss her.

She hardly knew kissing. Graydon—the only guy she'd ever had sex with—had stunk at it. He practically swallowed her. No finesse, no joy. She'd hated the taste of him, the way she'd had to wipe her mouth. But she'd always known kissing could be wonderful. How, she wasn't sure. Probably all the books she'd read. All the romantic movies. If that many people seemed to like it so much, there had to be something more to it.

Well, it wouldn't do her any good to think about that now. The best she could do was try and go out with some dignity. And pray that her father would survive the ordeal.

IT DIDN'T MATTER A damn to Ed Martini whether he threw two bodies or three overboard. All he wanted was to get the ransom money and get the hell out of town. At least until Sheila, that skinny bitch, stopped hawkin' him about her goddamn alimony. He'd thought about throwing her overboard, and while the idea made him happy, the police would be all over him in a heartbeat. Sheila'd made sure of that.

So he'd take the five million and go for a holiday. Maybe St. Thomas or even just the Keys. When he felt like it, he'd come back. Give the bitch her money. What would he care if he'd already covered his assets?

Ed looked over at the guy tied in the chair. He didn't recognize him, although something about him seemed familiar. Probably one of Sheila's hired detectives. Bitch.

"What's your problem?"

Ed turned to see Jazz poking Charlie in the shoulder. Charlie looked like he was gonna have a heart attack on the spot.

"What's your problem?" Jazz repeated.

"Nothin'. I'm just wondering when we can go get the ransom, you know?"

Jazz gave him another shot to the arm, but Charlie, he didn't seem to be so worried about the ransom as he was about the guy in the chair.

Ed leaned back in his leather chair, thinking maybe in a few minutes he'd have the cook bring up some dinner. A nice piece of salmon, maybe. "Jazz, get the guy's wallet."

Jazz—the only one in his whole outfit he could trust completely—bent next to the passed-out guy and took his wallet from his back pocket. He opened it up. "Michael Caulfield."

At the sound of his name, the man in question moaned and lifted his head. It fell back to his chest, but he tried again, and this time he succeeded.

"Hey, Charlie," Ed said. "You wanna explain to me why we have a man with your last name come to my boat with a gun in his hand?"

"I—I—"

"I'm the one that told him about Tate."

Ed looked at the brother. Except for the blood seeping down the side of his face, he looked a lot smarter than Charlie. Of course, a potato was smarter than Charlie.

"You did, huh? What exactly did you tell Charlie?"

The brother sniffed, wincing at that small movement. "I told him she was worth millions. That she was planning this fake kidnapping, so nobody would be the wiser if he was the one who took her."

"And you knew this because…?"

"I'm her bodyguard."

Ed smiled. It was just what Charlie had told them. "So, great, you told him. And he told me. You both did good. But now I think you both don't need to stick around."

"Wait a minute," Charlie said, his voice high and scared. "I'm supposed to help with the ransom, ain't I? Isn't that what you said? That I help with the ransom and then we're square? I didn't owe you five million dollars, Ed. I owed you hardly nothing compared to that. Tell him, Jazz."

Jazz moved over to the big leather chair and crouched down beside his boss. "You know, I don't care about the brother, but Charlie, we could still use him."

Ed leaned to his side, keeping his voice as low as Jazz had. "For what?"

"After we kill the others, after we get the money, we make sure the cops start sniffin' at Charlie. And before they catch him, he has an accident. And they don't sniff any further."

This was why Jazz got the big salary. He might look like your junkie cousin, but he was a smart spick. Always thinking. Ed gave him a slight nod, then turned to Charlie. "Relax. I was just kiddin'. Wasn't I, Jazz?"

"Yep, just kiddin'."

"About you, at least. I think you'll agree that your brother has served his purpose."

Charlie looked at his brother, then back at the two men. His eyes were wide, his nose was runny and he looked like he was gonna puke. "We don't have to kill him. He told me all about this deal, you know? We wouldn't even be here if it wasn't for Mikey."

"That's true, Charlie," Ed said, "but the man brought a gun into my home. That's very disrespectful. I'm sure you can see that."

"He didn't mean nothin' by it. I swear to God, Ed, he didn't mean to offend."

Ed sighed. "It's too late for apologies." He looked at his watch. It was almost eight-thirty. No wonder he was so hungry. He turned to his right and picked up the intercom that led to the galley. That's where the cook was. And the pilot, too. "Pauly?"

He waited a few beats, and just when he was going to speak again he heard, "Yes, boss?"

"You got some dinner ready?"

"Ten minutes, boss. You want something special?"

"If you have a nice piece of salmon, that would be good."

"Yes, sir."

"And, Pauly, make enough for..." He looked at Charlie and wished he'd go wash his face. But he'd feed the stupid bastard. Jazz, too. And he had to feed the woman because they might need her between now and when they got the money. "Make enough for four of us, okay?"

"Yes, sir. Right away."

He put the intercom down and nodded toward the small refrigerator in the bar.

Without a word, Jazz fetched him a beer. Opened it for him, put it down on a nice napkin on the little table next to the chair. Then Jazz turned on the TV that was mounted on the wall across from the table. There were four sets so Ed could watch a bunch of different games. He had to know where his money was coming from. That's why it didn't matter where this boat went—he could always be in touch with Ronnie at the office, via satellite. Ronnie, his eldest son, ran the day-to-day.

He took a big drink of the ice-cold brew, then waited for the burp. Once he was comfortable, he turned back to Jazz. "Kill him."

Jazz grinned and got out his gun. It was a .45, a birthday present from his old man.

"I didn't tell him everything," Michael said.

"Don't even try—"

"I didn't tell Charlie about the real money." The brother turned his head and looked at Ed. "The ransom is chicken feed. I know how to get fifty million. Tax-free. No one the wiser."

"Fifty million?" Jazz slapped his head just where he'd hit him before.

The brother hissed, but he didn't pass out.

"Hold on a minute, Jazz. Just what are you trying to tell me, Mr. Caulfield?"

The brother swallowed, blinked, then straightened his back. "The woman is worth ten times that. But the money I'm talking about is in a numbered account in the Cayman Islands. If you kill her now, you get five million. If you get her bank account number, fifty million gets transferred to your account. No questions. No taxes."

"And what do you want from this little deal?"

"You think I want to babysit a spoiled brat for the

rest of my life? I figure two hundred thousand in the Caymans? I'm a king."

Ed leaned forward, his interest definitely piqued. "Mr. Caulfield, I realize you told us this information to save your life. But I must ask—now that you have told us, what do we need you for?"

"I'm the only one who can get you that account number."

"And why would she do that for you?"

The brother smiled. "She's in love with me."

# 6

TATE TRIED TO FIGURE out how long it had been since they'd gotten her father's phone number. She didn't have her watch and she couldn't remember if she'd left home without it this morning or if they'd taken it from her. It had been dark the first time she'd been conscious, and it was still dark, so that didn't help.

She couldn't see much from where she lay. There was the low ceiling and the little port window. Across from the bed was a dresser and a small vanity table with chair. Everything was bolted down, of course. There were no loose objects anywhere. The lights, she'd seen when they had come on, were recessed. There were no table lamps.

There was also a second door. They'd come in and out of the one kitty-corner from the berth. This one, she had come to believe, led to the head. Which she would really like to use. Soon.

She still couldn't get over how calm she felt. Other, normal people probably wouldn't consider this calm, not with her still-pounding heart and the numbness in her limbs. But given her circumstances? She was doing damn well. She wasn't going to bet the farm that all her panic issues were resolved, but this was okay. This was survivable. Which was irony at its finest.

In between figuring out the second door and trying to hear if someone was coming, unwanted memories came to haunt her. The first kidnapping, not the second. The one that had cost her Lisa.

They'd been taken from Tate's bedroom. Lisa, her best friend and cousin, had spent the night, which was something they did often. The two of them had been held in a basement for two days. Somehow, for reasons that had eluded her and made guilt a part of every single day, she'd escaped. Lisa hadn't.

She froze again, listening hard. Nothing. She heard the lap of the waves against the boat, but even those were soft, barely audible. She heard her own breathing, too. But at least she could hear things over the pounding of her heart, which was an improvement.

She lifted her right leg, making sure to keep her cuffed arm as still as possible. It actually wasn't that bad. She was able to move without screaming or trying to slash her own artery so she'd bleed out.

Then she lifted the left leg. It worked as well as the right.

One of the things she had done in college was work her body. Thank goodness that, in addition to yoga and Pilates to keep herself limber, she'd taken those self-defense classes. She'd learned to shoot and shoot well. She'd done those things to make her feel courageous, and none of them had worked worth a damn.

But as of this afternoon her universe had changed. She wasn't sure if she would remember one thing she'd learned from any of her classes or if she'd just pass out again the moment the door opened, but she was going to move forward under the assumption that in this universe she kicked ass.

The first thing to do was to move her legs, stretch the muscles. It was vital that she had control over every part of her that still worked. One hand, two legs and a brain. With luck, she'd get in at least a few licks before they tossed her into the ocean.

"WHY SHOULD I BELIEVE YOU?"

Michael wished they'd undo the rope that was cutting him across the chest. Of course, if they did, the first thing he'd have to do was kill his brother.

Goddamn Charlie. He must have gotten into the safe when Michael had gone to his bedroom to change shirts. There was no other explanation, and for that, for this, whatever deal he'd made with his father, deathbed or no, he was through with Charlie. Assuming they both weren't killed in the next five minutes. "You should believe me because you're here. You think Charlie could have put this together?" He laughed and he wasn't the least bit sorry to see the look of hurt in Charlie's eyes.

"Speaking of being here, how did you find us?"

"I got that one covered, boss," Jazz said, holding up Michael's GPS.

"That's great, Jazz. What's he tracking?"

"The woman."

Ed Martini, who Michael deduced the tan gentleman to be, sighed. "What on the woman is he tracking?"

"Oh, crap."

"Want to share, Mr. Caulfield?"

He debated lying, but all they had to do was bring the GPS in proximity to Tate's purse and it was all over. "Her purse. It's wired."

"Jazz, ask Danny to come up, would you? Then have him take Miss Baxter's purse and dump it somewhere in New Jersey."

"Sure thing, boss."

Ed turned back to Michael. "I still don't see how you'd convince her to give you that number. You'd have to kill me and pretty much everyone I knew to convince me."

He looked back at Ed, willing himself not to move, not to do what his training had ingrained in him: escape. "Tate Baxter has been rich her whole life. The kind of rich that alters her perception of money. I think fifty million dollars is one hell of a lot. But when you've got over a hundred billion dollars in assets..."

Jazz whistled. "I knew she was loaded—"

"Look up the Baxter Corporation online," Michael said. "Look William Baxter up in the Forbes 500. He's the third wealthiest man in the United States, and that doesn't include his numbered accounts."

Michael forced himself to relax and to keep his mouth shut. The ball had been lobbed over the net, and he had to see whether they were going to put it in play.

He wished he'd thought of something smarter, something that would get them both off this boat tonight, but it wasn't a terrible plan. Ed Martini was a bookie, one of the biggest on the East Coast. He was a man who liked to play the odds. The potential of a ninety percent profit would appeal to the gambler in him.

What did he have to lose by checking it out? Michael knew Ed wasn't about to forget the five million. No one seemed to be in a huge rush to get it, so they either hadn't called in the ransom yet or they must have given William some time to gather the cash. Michael's whole objective was to buy time.

Eventually the circumstances for victory would come his way. This was the kind of thing he'd trained for all his adult life, and these guys? They knew nothing but the brute fundamentals. He'd win and he'd get Tate out of this in one piece. If they believed him right now.

"Yeah, that's all swell, but the five million, we don't need her for that. And there's no guarantee—"

"She's crazy about him, Ed," Charlie said. "You threaten to hurt Mikey and she'll do anything you want."

Ed barely gave Charlie a glance. "It seems like a lot of trouble."

"Not so much trouble," Michael said, "not fifty million dollars' worth. Completely untraceable."

"But if she signs over the money, she can just as easily blow the whistle."

Michael smiled at Jazz. "I don't see how, unless she can communicate from the other side."

Jazz's thin eyebrows came down as he frowned.

While Michael waited for him to *comprende,* he took a moment to think about a particularly juicy way he would kill the man when the time came.

"Oh. The other side. I get it."

"Once you know the account is legit and you make the transfer, there's no way anyone's going to trace the transaction. Not if you put the money back into the same bank under your name."

Ed chuckled just as the hatch opened at the front of the saloon. A bald guy came up the stairs. He stopped there and pulled a big tray filled with food up from the hold. Then another. Following the second tray there came a man in a white chef's coat.

Michael turned his attention back to the bald guy. He was older than Michael by at least a couple of years, but, shit, he was in great shape. Michael would need to bring a weapon along to kill that one.

Evidently he was Danny. The one who was going to lose the GPS tracker. Jazz made him wait as he went into the berth at the inside of the saloon. He came out again holding the Coach bag. Before he handed it to Danny, he took the cash out of Tate's wallet and her wristwatch.

Michael changed his mind. He would kill Jazz with a dull fish knife instead.

The chef was nothing. A chef. If this was everyone who would be on the boat, he could manage. There was only one guy who truly scared him and that was Jazz. Michael knew the type—he enjoyed his job. The more people he could hurt, the better.

The discussion was over, at least for now. As the chef and baldy set up the table for Ed's dinner, Ed finished his beer, then told Jazz to cut him loose.

"Take him into the cabin and cuff him next to his girlfriend."

Michael didn't show his relief. All he cared about now was making sure Tate was okay.

WILLIAM BAXTER STOOD in his upstairs closet, staring at the shelves of his safe. He'd never given much thought to the heft and weight of five million dollars, but he did so now. He knew, because it was important to know such things, that one million dollars in one hundred dollar bills weighed twenty-two pounds. Therefore, five million dollars would weigh one hundred and ten pounds. He needed a vessel, something he could fit into a public trash Dumpster, something that wouldn't look suspicious to someone passing by, something that would hold one hundred and ten pounds of hundred-dollar bills. It was a serious matter. One, if he got it wrong, that could mean his daughter's death.

His eyes closed as he tried to regain his bearings. He kept remembering the phone call. The electronically altered voice.

*Your daughter is ours. Bring five million in unmarked hundreds to the Central Park carousel. At two-thirty this morning put the cash in the Dumpster with the red X. No police. No tracking chip or dye packs. You deliver the money by yourself. One thing goes wrong, Tate is dead.*

He had to get a grip on himself. There was nothing he wouldn't do for his daughter, including giving these people his money. If only he could believe that following the instructions to the letter would be enough.

He knew only too well that if a man was capable of kidnapping, he was capable of murder.

It occurred to him that the vessel he was desperately searching for had been so obvious, if he hadn't been this close to tears. He would use an old gym bag. There were a couple downstairs.

But to go downstairs would telegraph that something was wrong. The last thing he needed was for the staff to gossip. Any oblique reference at all could be enough to cause damage.

He would have to call Stafford, his majordomo. Just as he stepped out of the closet, his intercom buzzed. His heart leaped in his chest, but he made it to the phone. "Yes?"

"Sara Lessing returning your call, sir."

"Yes. And, Stafford, please come to my room and bring one of those old gym bags from the storage room. Discreetly."

"Sir."

William pressed the lit phone line. "Sara."

"Hi, Mr. Baxter. Is something wrong?"

"Is Tate with you?"

"Uh, no."

"Would you happen to know where she is?"

"She didn't say anything to me about having plans."

"I see," he said, sitting down before his knees gave out. He hadn't realized how much stock he'd put in the idea that Tate was simply with her friend and this was all a prank.

"Mr. Baxter, have you tried her cell?"

"Yes. I have."

"What about Michael? Or Elizabeth? They'd know."

"Mr. Caulfield is also not available by phone, and Elizabeth suggested Tate was with him."

"Oh. Wait."

"Yes?"

"Okay, nothing's wrong. Not really. Except…well, I wasn't supposed to tell you…."

"Sara, please—"

"Of course. I'm sorry. Tate is participating in this, well, sort of stunt."

"Pardon me?"

As William listened to Tate's best friend outline the lunatic plan, every part of him wanted her words to be true. He hadn't wept since his wife died twenty-two years ago, but he wept now, knowing that the silly plan to fake Tate's kidnapping had gone so horribly wrong.

"Sir?"

"Thank you, Sara. I appreciate your explanation. However…"

"Yes?"

"An hour ago I received a ransom call."

Sara didn't say anything for a long time. "Michael is with her. He'll make sure she's safe. I know he went after her. He was against the whole idea."

"Was he?"

"Oh, God."

"I have to go. Needless to say, if you hear—"

"Of course. And if there's anything—"

"I'll call you." He hung up, and only then did Stafford enter the room, carrying a large black gym bag.

"Is this fine, sir?"

It was perfect. All five million dollars fit inside with just enough room to zip it closed. He had several hours to kill until the drop-off. Plenty of time to imagine the hell Tate was in.

THE DOOR OPENED AND all Tate's bravado vanished. Before she could even see who had opened it, she was hit by a massive panic episode. Heart, lungs, legs, brain…all the things she had counted on were no longer under her control. The fear had her tight and the room dimmed.

"Tate."

She opened her mouth, but his name wouldn't come.

"Tate, look at me."

The side of the bed dipped, and she felt his cool fingers on the side of her face. The tunnel vision, which blocked out so much, softened and let her see who it was. "Michael."

He smiled. He wasn't wearing his sunglasses, either, so she could see his eyes. "You're hurt."

"It's okay. You found me."

"I did."

"Thank you. I was so scared. I was sure… Is my father here?"

His smile sank and the light in his eyes went out. "Oh, Christ, Tate, I'm sorry. I can't take you home. Not yet."

"What?"

"Lover boy here is joining the party."

Tate looked just past Michael. The small man was there, leering at her as if her heartbreak was better than cable.

"I'm sorry. I followed you, but when I got to the boat, they found me."

"It's all right," she said, even though she could hardly understand. It was Michael, and he was supposed to save her.

He leaned down close. "Don't fret," he whispered. "I'll get you out of this. I promise."

"Come on, my dinner's getting cold."

Michael spun away from her and stood up to Jazz. "Get that cuff off her now so I can clean her up. In case you've forgotten, you still need her. Then, when she's clean and there's a bandage on that wrist, you can bring in our dinner."

For a moment it looked as if Jazz was going to shoot Michael, but then he burst out laughing. "Man, you got you some pair."

"Whatever. Just get the cuffs off her."

Her breathing grew more stable as each moment passed. Well, as long as she kept her gaze on Michael. He took her into the head to wash her wrist, but then he must have noticed her discomfort, because he left her there, closing the door behind him.

She trembled so violently it was difficult to do the most fundamental things, but she managed, and then Michael joined her again, washing her wrist as if she might break. Which, when she thought about it, was entirely possible.

"I know that has to sting like hell."

"It's okay. This is the best pain I've had since—"

"I let you down. I'm sorry."

"You couldn't have known. Brody has a great deal to answer for. He's behind this, you know. He might not be here, but he's the only one who knew about the plan, so it follows."

He didn't say anything, but she watched his lips narrow and become pale. Never, though, was his touch anything but gentle.

"Michael?"

"Yes?"

"Did they call my father?"

He turned off the small faucet and got her a towel from a silver bar on the wall near the enclosed shower. With the same care, he dried her. "Don't touch that," he said, nodding at the very red and raw flesh.

He looked in the cabinet above the sink, choosing a bottle of aspirin, then in another cupboard near the door he found a first-aid kit. "Let's go sit. I want you to eat."

"I'm not hungry."

"I don't care. You need to eat. To be strong."

She sighed. "No amount of food is going to help with that."

"Let's do this before our friend Jazz gets too antsy."

She followed him to the bed, where she blushed like a fool as she climbed to the middle of the mattress. This was, for all its horror, a very intimate situation. She'd had her fantasies about Michael, but his actual touch, the scent of his skin, the closeness was something she hardly knew how to handle.

The good part was her awkwardness with Michael kept her from thinking about her own imminent death.

"What's so funny?"

"Nothing. Do I have to put that stuff on?"

He held up the antibiotic ointment. "This? It doesn't hurt at all."

"Promise?"

He nodded. "Promise."

He was true to his word. It didn't hurt. His touch did, but she didn't mind. He'd clearly done this kind of thing before. Probably in the military. When it was a matter of life or death.

She was just about to question him about his medical training when Jazz walked in, gun out and aimed at Michael. Immediately behind him came a very large bald man carrying a tray.

"Where's this supposed to go?" The bald man sounded as if he was from the Bahamas or Jamaica.

Jazz seemed stumped, so Michael took over, setting the tray on the dresser, then setting a napkin in her lap, along with a fork and a dinner plate.

He brought his own over, and when he sat down on the edge of the bed, Jazz said, "Hey."

Michael looked up.

Jazz glanced from Michael's food to the other room.

"Get your plate. You can eat in here and shoot us if we don't pass the salt."

Jazz didn't think that was quite so funny. He walked over to Michael and pressed the barrel of the gun into the center of his forehead. "You wanna be careful there, buddy. There's a big ocean out there and a lot of hungry fish."

"Got it," Michael said. "I apologize."

"That's better."

Despite his anger, he did as Michael had suggested. He ate at the vanity, his gun within easy reach.

She did her best to ignore him as she ate. It was superb salmon. In fact, the whole meal was perfectly prepared, but it was still difficult to swallow.

She kept thinking about her father. About how scared he must be. Each time she started to slide to the bad place, she looked at Michael. It helped so very much.

# 7

CHARLIE WIPED HIS forehead, wishing like crazy he could get off this stinkin' boat. He needed a fix and he needed it now, but Mikey was in there with that skinny chick, and Ed, he wasn't feeling so generous.

He looked down at his plate, but there was no way he was gonna eat, even if it was all cooked by some fancy chef.

All he wanted was for them to get the ransom. Then he could leave and he wouldn't owe Martini any more money. Nothing. In fact, with his cut, he'd be able to set himself up just fine. Screw Mikey. He should have helped him, that's all. If he had helped, none of this would have happened. Goddamn, he'd promised Pop he'd help. Now they were both in it up to their necks.

"Charlie."

He wiped his forehead again, this time with his napkin instead of his sleeve, then turned to face Ed. Jazz was in the other room with Mike and the skinny chick. So it was just him and Ed. "Yeah, Ed?"

"Charlie, why didn't you tell me about the bank account in the Caymans?"

Shit, shit and more shit. He didn't like answering

questions. Especially when the wrong answer could get him killed. "I didn't know."

"Your brother didn't tell you?"

"He told me about the kidnapping thing, right? About how she was paying somebody to snatch her. And he told me she was worth, you know, a lot of money. And that's what he told me."

"Nothing about the bank account."

Charlie shook his head. "He doesn't always tell me everything. He thinks he so damn smart and that I'm just his loser brother."

"He never mentioned that he was going to follow you?"

"He might have. I don't know. Maybe not."

"Tell me more about him. Has he been her body-guard for a long time?"

"Hell, no. Only about six months. Since he got out of the Army."

"He was in the military?"

"Yeah. Some big shit. They all kissed his ass."

"Why isn't he still some big shit?"

Charlie felt his cheeks heat. He didn't want to tell this part, but Ed would know if he was lying. "Because of me."

"Really? What happened?"

"I, uh, took some things from one of his Army friend's car one time."

"Things?"

"Some papers about a weapon or something. I'm not even sure what they were. They were just in this locked briefcase, so I figured they must be worth something. I didn't get to sell it, though. They caught me and I did some time. He said he was through with me, but I'm his brother, you know? He promised he'd look after me."

"I see."

"Anyway, I was wondering…what time are we gonna get the ransom? Because I have some, you know, things I gotta do."

"Not for several hours, Charlie. Just finish your dinner, and I'll let you know when we're going to leave."

He nodded, turned back to his plate. But now he was even less hungry. Damn that Mikey. He shoulda helped out his only brother.

FINALLY, JAZZ LEFT. He turned off the light and he locked the door behind him, but they were finally alone.

"I know," Tate said, shaking the cuff against the bar. "It's really uncomfortable."

After dinner, Jazz had cuffed him right next to her. They were lying down with plenty of pillows behind them. He'd even gotten Jazz to cover them with a blanket. But there was no way he was going to be this uncomfortable for the whole night.

"Tell me something, Tate. What is it you like about that Prada store?"

She didn't say anything for a minute, then she giggled. Tate was not the giggling type. It sounded pretty good on her.

"It's not that I like the store so much. I know people there and I like the way their clothes look on me. What are you doing?"

He had gotten his comb out of his left back pocket and was now inching his way up the bed to get in the best position. They'd hooked him up with his right hand, unfortunately, but his left would do.

As soon as he could maneuver properly, he pressed the far edge of the comb down on the pawl. It took him a while to disengage the pawl from the ratchet, but once that was done, the cuff popped open.

"Was that what I think it was?"

He followed the same steps with her handcuff. He left both cuffs hanging from the bar as he moved down and closer to Tate.

"How did you do that?"

"My uncle was Houdini."

"Really?"

"No. I wasn't always a limo driver."

"I know. You were a spy."

"Sort of."

"Why sort of?"

He moved even closer to her and decided he'd better just go for broke. "Lift up." He tapped her on the back of her neck.

She did, and he slipped his arm in back of her, cradling her head.

"I was in military intelligence, which is, yeah, the spy division. We broke into places, stole information, coordinated military operations and the CIA presence."

"Sounds terrifying."

"It could be. But when I say I was well trained, I'm not kidding."

"Why in the world aren't you still there? Doing important things?"

"Taking care of you is important."

"Oh, please. I'm a spoiled rich girl with psychiatric issues. How important can I be?"

"To me?"

She didn't respond except for a little shiver. Good. He didn't want her to be scared. He wanted her to believe that he could get them out of this. If not tonight, then in the near future. He needed her to do whatever he asked of her, no matter what. And for that she needed to be panic-attack-free.

It would all be so much easier if his own brother wasn't sitting in the next room. What killed him was that he'd let Charlie get the better of him again. The first time had cost him his military career. This time it would cost a hell of a lot more. He couldn't even blame his brother. Charlie was Charlie. Nope, this was his own damn fault, and before he got fired, quit, whatever, he was going to make damn sure Ed Martini and Jazz would never bother anyone again. He would make sure that none of the Baxter money was taken and he'd do whatever the hell it took to make sure Tate Baxter went home safely.

"Michael?"

"Yes?"

"Is something wrong?"

"No. No, I'm just angry at myself. I should never have let you go into that store alone."

"I wasn't alone."

"But Elizabeth—"

"Is amazingly capable. She isn't at fault. I won't have her lose her job over this."

He smiled, glad she couldn't see him. "Okay. Elizabeth stays."

"Good."

"Speaking of good, you're doing damn well yourself."

"Not really." She snuggled in closer, and he was glad to have her warmth. "I passed out. Several times."

"Understandable."

"And when I was conscious, I was in full panic mode. I didn't do any of the stuff I was trained to do."

"It's a whole different ball game when it's for keeps."

"I'm just sorry, that's all."

"For what? None of this is your fault."

"I don't know. Maybe all these years of focusing so much energy into my fear of being kidnapped…"

"You did not bring this on."

She sighed, and he felt a small drop of wet on his shoulder.

"Talk to me, Tate. I've heard…"

"That I'd been kidnapped?" she asked. "That we— me and my cousin—were taken from my bedroom?"

He wasn't sure if he should push or just let it go. Maybe talking about it would help, but he was no psychiatrist. Of course, she'd probably told Dr. Bay about this, but Dr. Bay, he now knew, was an ass.

He nodded, squeezed her shoulder.

"Her name was Lisa. She was my best friend. My only friend. Because her father and mine worked together and we were the same age. We did everything together."

"Same age, huh?"

"Yep. Her mother—my aunt Sharon—made sure we stuck close because my mother died when I was two."

"I didn't know you were that young."

"I don't remember much about her. But I remember everything about my childhood with Lisa."

"Tell me about it."

"She had really long hair and I used to love to brush it. I would pretend I was a hairdresser and we'd play every day. I was sure that's what I was going to be when I grew up."

"You? A hairdresser?"

"Why not?"

"I can't picture it."

"Back then, when we were little kids, we weren't really rich. Not like we are now. My father and his brother had gotten some lucrative government contracts, which is basically what made the company, but we were as nouveau as it gets. We were so happy. We traveled, we explored. Lisa and I did everything together. We were as close as sisters."

"What happened?"

"We were fifteen. So that's—"

"Nine years ago."

She nodded and her hair brushed against his neck.

"Since we traveled so much to places like Italy, England, Spain, we'd been taught to be really careful there because of all the kidnappings. Lisa and I barely thought about it, but there was always someone watching out for us. Damn, it was fun. I never felt lonely. We had the same tutors and the same homework. We wore the same clothes. We actually didn't look that much alike, but everyone thought we were twins."

"Sounds great."

"It was."

That little shiver he'd felt just a few moments ago was back, but it meant something completely different now. He'd seen her tremble just before a panic attack. Just before her breathing became labored and her skin turned deathly pale. He'd meant for the conversation to relax her, to help her trust him. Not send her into a tailspin.

"I never had anyone I was real close to when I was a kid," he said. "I was into sports, mostly football, but I kept having to change schools."

"Why?"

"My old man was a drunk. We had to skip on the rent at least once a year."

"Oh, my God."

"Yeah, well. He was the reason I signed up for the Army, so I guess it wasn't so bad."

She turned to look at him. It was so dark in the room he couldn't make out her expression, although he had a good idea what it was. "Wasn't so bad? I can't believe you're so cavalier about it."

"I've lived with it all my life. One adjusts."

"I don't think it's nearly that easy."

"You've adjusted."

"No, I haven't. That's the whole point. I should have adjusted years ago. I should have put my fear in the proper perspective. I mean, come on, what are the odds that—"

He heard her take a swift breath, then laughter. Not giggling this time but the real thing.

"What's so funny?"

Her answer was delayed as she got herself under control. "What are the odds," she said, "that I'd get kidnapped three times?"

He grinned. "I'd say they were pretty good."

"Yep."

He stroked her hair, which was softer than he'd even imagined. "Well, the odds of you getting kidnapped four times have to be astronomical. So once this is over you're home-free."

She laughed again, and he joined her, and it was maybe the best thing that could have happened. Her whole body relaxed. Hell, at this rate, she might actually get some sleep tonight. They both needed to eat, sleep, stretch. He had no idea when opportunity would knock, and they both had to be ready.

He thought about getting up, but then her hand went to his chest and he realized she hadn't finished her story.

"Anyway," she said, her voice softer now, "we were really careful in Europe but not so much back home. It wasn't that no one thought anything could happen to us, but—"

"Home turf. It's hard to stay diligent."

She nodded. "We spent the night at each other's houses all the time. The night they took us we were at my place. It was summer, hot. I wasn't a big fan of the air conditioner, so I had my bedroom window open. It was nice to feel the breeze."

"Sure," he said.

"I remember a hand over my mouth. It smelled like stale cigarettes. We were dragged out the window in the middle of the night. Both of us were blindfolded, gagged and tied up. We were thrown in the back of a truck. We rode for a long time and then we were carried inside, down some stairs. It was a basement, and it smelled like cigarettes and beer.

"It gets fuzzy after that. I only remember a few things. Lisa screaming. Someone taking off my nightgown. Praying. Then I was on a street I didn't recognize and I was wrapped in a white sheet. I was alone."

"You escaped."

"I got out, but I don't know if I had anything to do with it. Someone could have put me there, for all I know."

She wasn't shaking. Her voice was steady. Even her skin felt warm and dry. Had she told the story that many times? Or would she fall apart if he said a wrong word?

"I saw a woman in a window and I went to her door. She called the police."

"Lisa wasn't so lucky."

"No. She wasn't. They found her body three days later in a field that was covered with junk. They hadn't bothered to dress her, they just dumped her like so much trash."

"Tate—"

"It's okay. It's good to remember. To focus on the fact that it isn't over until it's over."

He pulled her close, resting his cheek on her soft hair. "There's nothing fair or good about any of it," he whispered. "I hope the bastards burn for eternity."

"Yeah," she said.

He rubbed her arm with his fingers, a very light, hypnotic touch. They didn't speak, and she didn't weep, but all the same the next hour was about calming down. About coming back to now.

When finally she sighed, he knew he could do what he had to do, even if it meant leaving her. Not for the whole night but for as long as it took him to do some recon. He'd been too busy fixing her wrist to really check out the bathroom. He was sure he would find something in there he could use as a weapon. Then there was the vanity and the dresser. Probably closets, too, although he didn't remember seeing them.

He looked over at the door, and there was still light coming in around the edges. Which meant if he turned on the light in here, it wouldn't be noticed.

"Tate, I have to move. I'm just going into the head. Will you be all right?"

The hand on his chest lifted slowly. "I'll be fine."

"I'm sorry, but I have to do this now. The light's still on in the saloon."

"Ah. That makes sense."

"I won't be long." He climbed out of the bed and went to the door. Even though he knew it was locked, he tried it anyway. Mistakes happened, and sometimes not by him. "Close your eyes," he said. "Light."

As soon as his eyes adjusted, he went to the vanity. This cabin was clearly used to accommodate women. He found a hairbrush, a mirror, makeup, creams, sprays. Nothing particularly helpful.

There were clothes in the dresser—women's, and some of them were mighty skimpy.

The head, however, held his interest. A package of safety razors. Those could come in handy. A long pair of scissors. Some isopropyl alcohol and a book of matches along with a scented candle. He could work with this stuff. He just had to be careful how and when, because Tate was his weakest link. He wouldn't allow them to use her as a bargaining tool, so he'd have to make damn sure if he struck, he'd win.

There was also the question of Charlie. Yes, he

wanted to kill him for his role in all this, but truthfully he wasn't sure he could, so there was another weak link.

If it had been just him, he'd have had no problem with the crew. He could get rid of Jazz in two shakes. The man was a brute, nothing more. But the bald guy, he might be trouble. The chef was no big deal, and Martini was too used to letting others do the dirty work.

But it wasn't just him. Tate's safety overruled everything.

He rearranged some of the equipment in the head, then he leaned out and said, "Just one more sec," before he closed the door with his foot.

After he'd washed, he went back into the cabin. Tate was still in the same position, the blue blanket pulled up above her breasts, her head resting on a mound of pillows. She looked pale and scared, but she hadn't simply been resting, waiting for him to return.

There was a fierceness about her he'd never seen before. Curious. Was it the talk of her little cousin? Or was it the laughter that had brought her a few steps closer to fighting back?

"What's that smile for?" she asked.

He hadn't realized. "You've made a decision."

"Pardon?"

"Nothing. It's not important." He turned off the lights and was once again amazed at the depth of the darkness.

"Are you going to be able to find your way back?"

"Eight steps," he said.

"Now that sounds like something a spy would say."

He got back to the bed and climbed in, shifting until he had her comfortably beside him again. "Those kinds of details make all the difference. Next time you go to the head, count. And when Jazz comes into the room, watch him. Does he go to the right or the left? Is he ready before he turns on the light or does he take a few seconds to adjust?"

Her hand touched his chest again. "Is it always like that for you? Everywhere?"

"Most of the time, yes."

"So how do you relax?"

He chuckled. "Well, there are a couple of ways…."

There was that little shiver again.

"I have a confession."

"Oh?"

"I've been meaning to invite you for dinner."

"Really?" Of course, he'd known about that for months, but he wasn't going to spoil this moment for her.

"I've always enjoyed our talks. I thought it would be nice to spend some time with you off the clock."

"It sounds nice."

"I know. Unfortunately I'm a big chicken. I was afraid you'd—"

"What?"

"I don't know. Just afraid."

"We're here now. And I don't see a clock anywhere."

Her hand moved. Not much and not under his shirt, but it was a start.

He stroked her hair once more and, as he did so, pulled her tighter against him. It wouldn't be easy to kiss her in such a dark place. He could miss by a mile. Unless…

He took her chin in his left hand and held her steady as he lowered his lips onto hers.

# 8

TATE'S EYES FLUTTERED closed at the whisper of his lips. She held her breath waiting for him to pry her mouth open, for the gaping maw that was all she'd known of kisses. But he barely touched her. Just a brush, an *almost* that made her quiver. She tried to remain still, to let him show her what he wanted, but the way he teased her, nearly touching, made her arch forward.

Even then, even with him truly kissing her, he was soft and deliberate. As if he were testing, putting his proverbial toe in the water.

The metaphor made her smile, and when he smiled in return, she felt it. Felt his lips curve and his warm breath mingle with hers.

A moment passed, and he must have decided that the water was fine because there was no more teasing. He took her mouth and his tongue slipped inside. In that instant she realized everything she'd known about kissing in the past was wrong.

He didn't swallow her whole or do anything that would spoil the moment. With his arm holding her head, his fingers still guiding her chin, she felt amazingly, astonishingly safe.

How was it possible to have the worst and best experience of her life happen at the exact same time?

Gathering her courage, she touched his tongue, and that was a sensation beyond thrilling. He let her lead the dance for a moment, then he was in charge once more.

She didn't mind. In fact, all she wanted was to surrender completely, let herself fall into this, into her dream become flesh.

He pulled away, only to return, nipped her bottom lip, then soothed her with the flat of his tongue. Kissing was wonderful. Better even than in her feverish imagination.

He moaned with his passion and hunger, and she laughed, it was so good. She'd made him moan. This sexy, experienced man of the world.

"What's so funny?"

"Nothing."

"Are you okay?"

She sighed. "I'm perfect." Then she kissed him.

He pulled her closer, and now that he had her, he let go of her chin to stroke her hair, to touch her cheek. Just as she pulled back to bare her neck, the door opened, throwing light all over the bed.

Tate jerked away as if she'd been caught doing something nasty.

"Hey, what the hell?" Michael said, leaning forward to block her from the intruder.

"Sorry to break up the party, but— What the—?" Jazz rushed to the side of the bed and held up the empty cuff. "Are you kidding me?"

"They were uncomfortable," Michael said.

"I'll show you uncomfortable." Jazz shoved his gun into the side of Michael's cheek. "Get up. Now."

Without moving, Michael said, "Tate, you just relax, okay? I'll be right back."

"I wouldn't count on it," Jazz said.

Despite the immediacy of the threat, Michael moved off the bed with incredible grace. The moment he stood, Jazz poked him in the ribs with his gun. "Cuff her."

"She's not going anywhere."

"Cuff her or I'll do it."

Michael obeyed, and her hand was once more above her head in a position that simply couldn't be comfortable. That was the least of her problems. Where were they taking Michael? God, what if he didn't come back?

"Please, can you tell me what's going on?" she asked.

"Shut the fuck up—that's what's going on." Jazz made Michael take his cuff off the metal bar, then Jazz cuffed his hands behind his back.

"I'll be back," Michael said. "You just get some rest."

She would have laughed if she'd had any control over her breathing. Or her heartbeat. It was all she could do not to beg Jazz to let him go, and when they left the room, slamming and locking the door behind them, she fell apart.

ED WAS STILL IN HIS big chair, but the dishes were gone. There were navigation charts on the table, two different cell phones, a laptop and a bottle of champagne in a silver ice bucket.

Ed looked up when Michael was pushed in front of his chair. "What was all that?"

"They were out of the cuffs."

Ed's gaze moved to Michael. "Really?"

"It's a handy parlor trick."

"I'll remember that. Do you have the account number?"

"No."

"Why not?"

"It's too soon. I need some time."

"You don't have time."

"Look, it doesn't matter if you have the account number. You can't get the money without Tate. She has to be there in person to sign the papers or the bank won't transfer that amount of money."

Ed just stared at him. He didn't move or frown or anything. "Jazz, uncuff him."

Jazz seemed affronted by the idea, but the keys came out and Michael was soon rubbing his wrists.

"You go back in there and you make sure this lady is going to do everything we need her to do. If she doesn't, we'll kill Charlie. Then her. Then you."

"TATE? CAN YOU HEAR me?"

Tate blinked as she pulled in an inadequate breath.

"I'm back. I said I would be back and I am. Can you look at me, Tate?"

It felt as if she were swimming up from the bottom of the ocean. There was light up there and warmth and safety, but it was so very far away.

"Come on, honey. You can do it. You're all right. Nothing's going to hurt you tonight. I'll be here the whole time and I won't let anything happen to you."

She jerked her hand again. She wasn't sure if she was trying to get loose or if she just needed the pain to jar her out of her nightmare.

"Shit, you're bleeding again. We need to get you to the bathroom so I can change the bandage."

"Michael?"

"I'm right here, Tate."

"They took you and I thought—"

"I know. But I promised—and I don't break my promises."

She focused. He was right next to her. The overhead lights were on, so she could see he wasn't hurt. And he wasn't cuffed. "What did you promise them?"

He sat back. "What?"

"What did you promise them? It's okay. I know you had to tell them something or they would have killed you."

"You're right. I did. I needed to buy us some time."

She could feel the real world become solid around her. The pace of her heart slowed, the tunnel vision expanded. It occurred to her that Michael had become her new safe place.

"I told them you have a numbered account in the Cayman Islands. That I was going to persuade you to give me the account number and that Martini would be able to transfer fifty million of your money into his account."

She thought about what he'd said for a moment. She could see the logic. If they thought they could get that much money, her life became a lot more valuable. "Actually, you're right. I do have a numbered account at the Grand Cayman Bank. But there's no way he can make that transfer. Not if I don't sign the papers in person."

"I was right?"

She nodded. "I'm surprised you're surprised. I figured a spy like you would know all about my finances."

"I don't know anything about them. It's not germane. Well, it wasn't until a few hours ago."

"Is that going to botch the deal? The fact that I have to sign the papers?"

"No. In fact, I think it can work in our favor. I'm pretty sure they're getting the ransom tonight. They're not going to be reckless about it, either. There's no way we're getting off this boat just yet. But if Ed believes you have to sign, then we've got all the way to the island to perfect our escape."

"I don't know about you," she said, "but I'm not that good a swimmer."

"He's going to have to get fuel, supplies. There will be opportunities."

"I don't know…. Remember what Jazz said— there's a big ocean and a lot of hungry fish."

"The man who kidnapped you is Ed Martini. He's one of the biggest bookies in the States. For fifty million dollars he's not going to take any chances. You'll be fine."

"Until I sign the papers."

"It won't come to that."

"I'd like to believe you."

"I came back, didn't I?"

She smiled. "Yes. You did."

"What do you say we get that bandage changed."

WILLIAM CHECKED HIS watch again as he drove slowly along the Sixty-fifth Street traverse. In a few minutes he would be at the carousel, and a few minutes after that he'd put the bag full of money in the red bin.

The drive in itself had been terrifying. He hadn't been behind the wheel in four years, and that had been in England. It meant nothing. To get his daughter back he would have walked here on his hands.

He'd obeyed the kidnapper's instructions to the letter, but after his discussion with Sara, he knew that someone from inside his organization had to be involved. He would deal with the incredible idiocy of the whole concept of fake kidnappings later. For now, he was looking at Michael Caulfield as the most likely traitor.

Sara's conviction that he would never do anything to hurt Tate was simply another nail in his coffin. William had hired Caulfield because he was supposed to be the very best at what he did. But he hadn't paid enough attention to why the man had been discharged. There was the whole unsavory business with the brother.

There was no question that he would get to the bottom of this. There was also no question that whoever had taken his daughter would pay with his life.

He had already passed the dark and shuttered Tavern on the Green. Everything was closed at this hour. However, the carousel was still illuminated. He would have preferred softer lights with some character to them, but these lamps weren't to entrance, they were to scare off the drug users and the teenagers who looked for dark corners to get their thrills.

He had to get close to the red-crossed trash bin. Not because of the instructions but because five million dollars was heavy and he wasn't a strong man. He wished he had followed his doctor's advice about exercise.

None of it would matter if he didn't get his girl back. He'd gone all these years with her safety as his vanguard. No matter where they'd traveled he'd spared no expense. Without Tate, he had nothing.

There it was. The only red-marked trash receptacle near the carousel. Though it was large, he'd have to work at getting the bag inside.

He parked the borrowed Cadillac. Stafford had wanted to drive it himself, but William had to do this alone. At least the Cadillac was easier to maneuver than his limousine. Once outside, he took the key to the trunk and lifted the lid. The gym bag was securely zipped. No casual passerby would think it contained blood money.

He took in a deep breath and hauled the bag up and over the rim of the trunk. Staggering as he walked the few steps to the marked bin, he had to rock his body so the bag would hit the opening.

After a moment to catch his breath, he shoved the bag into the bin until the whole thing fell. And fell.

He looked down, bracing his hands on the edge of the bin. There was no bottom. There was a trash-bin-size hole dug through the cement and the earth beneath. But all William could see was the end of his world.

WITH HER NEW BANDAGE and the comfort in knowing she wouldn't have to be cuffed again at least for the rest of the night, Tate finished up in the bathroom, grateful there were guest toiletries, including a couple of toothbrushes still in their boxes. She wasn't crazy about using the soap on her face, but as she washed she realized just how insane that was.

She was still alive when it could have so easily gone the other way. In fact, not much about this kidnapping had turned out like her fears.

Because of Michael.

She stared into the small mirror above the sink, wincing at the woman who looked back. Her eyes were red and puffy, as were her cheeks. She looked as if she'd been through hell. She had looked like this when he'd kissed her, and now it felt quite suspicious. Had he just been trying to keep her distracted? Calm her down? Probably. Shouldn't she mind a lot more?

Of course, she'd clearly gone quite mad when the truth had penetrated that she'd really been kidnapped. How insane does a person have to be to worry that her new potential boyfriend might not like her skin tone when on the brink of death? If they lived through this, she would definitely need a new therapist.

Well, she couldn't stay in the head all night. It just seemed so odd that he was out there. That they would be sharing a bed.

That sucked her breath right out of her lungs.

They were sharing a bed. It might be her last night on Earth. The math wasn't difficult. She thought of the kisses and how it had felt to finally have a real man want her. Even if it was all an act, she didn't care. As far as last wishes went, this was a good one.

A shudder shook her body as once again reality and delusion smacked into each other. This was so different than anything she'd imagined—and she'd imagined so much. In her nightmares there was no rest, no relief from the terror. There was certainly no kissing and no trust that somehow she'd survive.

A tap on the door sent her heart into overdrive.

"Tate? You okay?"

"I'm fine," she said. "I'll be out in a minute."

He needed to brush his teeth, to get himself ready for bed. Although she'd like to, she couldn't stay here for the rest of the night.

She took one last glance in the mirror—which was not terribly smart, considering—then went into the small bedroom.

Michael stood by the door, an easy smile on his lips. Part of her ease with him was a conditioned response. Michael only took off his sunglasses when they were having their wonderful conversations. The more she connected with his gaze, the calmer she felt.

"You need something?" he asked. "There are some clothes in the drawers. Maybe you could find yourself something more comfortable to wear."

She couldn't. The idea of wearing someone else's things…

"I'll be out in a minute. The door's locked. You'll know if someone's trying to come in."

She looked at the door, then back at Michael. Selfishly she wished he didn't have to go, even for a few minutes. "I'll be fine."

"I know," he said. A moment later he was in the head and she was alone. Only it didn't feel quite so bleak.

She went to the dresser and opened the top drawer. Bikinis. Many of them. All so tiny they made her blush. Second drawer down had cover-ups, but they were mostly transparent. God, what must go on in this boat.

She shook her head at her prudishness. She'd been around a lot of sex in her life, even though she hadn't been the one having it. In her fancy prep school she'd spent many a night wearing headphones so she wouldn't have to hear the grunting coming from the other bed.

In college things had gotten more personal. Graydon had taken her to parties where the drugs and alcohol had flowed like water. Inhibitions were nonexistent, and she'd become inured to the sight of her fellow students going at it like bunnies.

But then she'd retreated to her world of fear, and so much of the outside world had taken on sinister tones. At the very least it had become unfamiliar. More real by far was her fantasy life. It was in bed she truly lived. That's where all her plans were, her dreams. And that's where sleeping with Michael made sense.

She breathed deeply, closed her eyes. Pictured herself as a warrior, complete with combat boots and semiautomatic weapon. A minute of positive self-talk and she got into bed.

If she'd known she was going to be kidnapped, she would have dressed differently. Certainly she wouldn't have worn the linen pants. But this was what she had and she'd cope. By tomorrow… No, she wasn't going to think about tomorrow. Her only decision at the moment was about her shoes.

They were pumps, two-inch heels. Great for shopping at Prada, lousy for self-defense—but better than her bare feet. The idea of sleeping in them was disconcerting.

Nothing to be done about it. She lifted the pillows and pulled back the comforter. The blanket Jazz had brought wasn't terribly warm, and as long as they could be comfortable, she supposed they should be.

Fully dressed, she climbed into the bed and pulled up the covers. She plumped the strange, too-firm pillow beneath her head and closed her eyes.

This was going to be one long uncomfortable night.

She sighed at the absurd thought. What, was she expecting a designer kidnapping?

Well, that made her laugh because, yes, that's exactly what she'd expected. Designed to her exact specifications with three gourmet meals a day and furry handcuffs and a stop to it all at her first whim.

God, she was some piece of work.

"Tate?"

She looked up to find Michael standing by the bed. He was clearly concerned at her outburst, but he'd also caught her contagious laughter, so he was grinning, too.

Which made everything funnier. By a lot.

"Tate," he said, trying hard to keep his cool. "What's going on?"

"I'm a first-class twit," she said, although she doubted he understood her because she really couldn't stop laughing.

"You're a what?"

The way he looked at her, so shocked his eyes had widened and he was actually blushing, let her know he'd misunderstood. She struggled once more to get some decent breaths. "What did you think I said?"

"Nothing that you would ever say."

Then she got it. "I said *twit*."

"Aah. Much better."

That was it. She was crying now. Laughing so hard her stomach ached.

He sat down, grinning and shaking his head.

It was just the kind of scene she'd dreamed of, in her bed, alone, in the dark. Everything about him was perfect. The situation wonderful, like something out of a Nora Ephron romantic comedy. Except for the danger that hovered a whisper away.

Before she could catch her breath, he was next to her under the covers and she was in his arms.

# 9

SHE TREMBLED IN HIS arms, and all he could think about was going into the saloon and killing everyone on the boat. Maybe that's what he should do—end this thing right now. Of course, he had no idea what kind of weapons were stashed up there. He could take Jazz out, but it was more than a fair bet that Ed had a gun on him, and he wouldn't hesitate to kill everyone in front of him. Martini didn't get to be in his position without a lot of buried bodies.

Despite Michael's fury at his brother, he didn't want Charlie to die. And Charlie would go down first, there wasn't much doubt about that. As terrible as it sounded, he'd be willing to risk it if it meant getting Tate off the boat and to safety.

That was the wild card. In the old days he'd never consider pulling off a job with so many unknowns. That was how people got killed. Before he'd take out a position, be it a hostage takeover of a plane, a bunker or a terrorist cell, he and his men would know everything there was to know about the targets. There were always risks, but his job was to minimize them, not subject this terrified woman to living her last moments in her worst-case scenario.

"It's okay, Tate," he whispered. "I'm here. I won't leave you. I won't let them hurt you."

"I'm sorry," she whispered, her voice muffled against his chest.

"No need to apologize."

She sniffled, then moved her head so her mouth wasn't pressing against him. "I keep thinking I'm fine, that I've got it under control."

"You've been doing great."

"For the record, you were right. The fake kidnapping was a lousy idea."

"Yeah, and this one's not so hot, either."

She sighed, her body shuddering with the exhalation. "I'm really worried about my father."

"He'll be busy trying to find us. Besides, he's a tough old man. He's dealt with dangerous circumstances before."

"That's what's got me so concerned. When my cousin was kidnapped, my uncle Joseph did everything he was supposed to. He didn't call the cops, he got all the money together and took it where they told him to. He followed their instructions to the letter. Once the kidnappers took the cash, they didn't give Lisa back. She was found three days later."

"Shit."

"She was fifteen. They'd hurt her, raped her. Then they killed her. Strangled her to death. Nothing was ever the same again."

"I thought you were—"

"I was. I escaped. I have no memory of it. None. I don't know why I got out and she didn't."

Michael didn't know what to say. No wonder Tate

was so phobic about being taken. She had every reason to be terrified. And because of him there was a damn good chance she was going to die, just as her cousin had.

He had to tell her about Charlie. No matter what, he couldn't let her find out on her own. It wasn't that he didn't relish facing her anger and disappointment; he deserved everything she could dish out. The problem was that she was hanging on by a thread here, and the only reason she hadn't lost it completely was because she trusted him.

Telling her that his own brother had given her over to the ruthless bastards out there was going to be a heavy blow. He had no clue if she'd be able to recover from it.

On the other hand, unless they got off the boat in the next few hours, it would be inevitable that she'd find out. Jazz and Ed—hell, even Charlie—had no reason to keep his secret.

He had no choice. He had to get them off this boat. In order to do that, he needed Tate to sleep. It was already late, and he didn't want to wait until everyone was fresh in the morning. His window of opportunity was in the next couple of hours.

Unfortunately he had no convenient means of helping Tate get some rest. No pills, no booze. He certainly wasn't going to knock her out.

"What's wrong?"

He looked down and met her gaze. "Nothing."

"I felt your whole body tense. What aren't you telling me?"

The urge to confess about Charlie hit him hard, but he held back. "You need to get some rest."

"That's not news. For that matter, so do you."

"You're right. So why don't we both try to sleep?"

Her quiet little laugh made her lips vibrate against his chest. "I have insomnia on good days. You think I'm going to be able to nod off here?"

He brushed the side of her face with his fingers, then lifted her chin so he could see her once more. "There are other ways to forget about what's out there."

She studied him while he took deep breaths. He probably shouldn't do this. It would add insult to injury when she found out about Charlie. But if he did it right, sex should put her right to sleep.

Not that the job would be difficult. He was already getting hard at the thought of touching her. He wanted to make her come so hard she'd pass out. Well, at least fall asleep. The trick would be not coming himself.

He liked to think he could be ready for anything, anytime, anyplace, but even he had to admit that there were certain circumstances… If she'd been a stranger or one of his friends who didn't think twice about hooking up for a night, there'd be no problem. But he liked Tate. He also knew that this wasn't a woman who took making love lightly.

The last thing he wanted to do was mess her up in this area, too. Jesus, he couldn't believe how screwed up this all was. He'd had an outstanding record his entire time in the service. Commendations, promotions. He'd led men into fights with no chance of success, only to come out the other end bloodied but unbowed.

Now he was on the cushiest job he'd had since college,

and it was fucked up beyond all reason. The worst of it was that Tate was the one paying for his mistakes.

"Michael?"

He reached down until he had a grip on her, then drew her up so she shared his pillow. He kissed her, wanting to make this as good as he could. He wanted her to know how he admired her, how beautiful she was and how extraordinary.

He might have had his fair share of terrific women, but Tate…Tate was different. Tate was—

MICHAEL TOOK HER mouth desperately. She came alive inside, kissing him back, clutching at his neck in her need to get closer.

It was like drowning in a riptide, being tugged under by forces so elemental there was simply no fighting back. She didn't want to fight.

Yes, *they* were out there, but in here she was being caressed by large, warm hands. He pulled his arm from underneath her neck so he could get at her buttons, and she reached for his. Inelegant—in fact, clumsy—they managed somehow to take off each other's tops and do some serious French kissing at the same time. It would make an interesting Olympic event, one she'd like to train for.

Her bra was off and she wasn't sure how. All she knew was that she liked the way her breasts felt as they pressed against his chest. Even better was his hand cupping her, brushing her very sensitive nipples before he squeezed her flesh.

Giddy with sensation, she ran her hand down his chest and stomach, amazed at the hardness of him, then down his pants, where she discovered a whole different kind of hardness. He was impressive. Not so big she'd walk funny but large enough she'd fill her diary with exclamation points. He was straining against his pants, hissing as she rubbed him.

Braver still, she found his zipper and managed somehow not to hurt him as she lowered it. Inside was her surprise. Hard, hot, thick, the moment her hand circled his shaft, his cock jumped as if he couldn't contain his eagerness.

"God, Tate," he murmured, his moan as deep as his thrusting tongue.

She loved touching him, but her hold was awkward, so she released him and tackled his belt.

That needed a more deft hand than her own, and being attentive, Michael pitched in. A moment later his pants were halfway off, leaving her feeling quite overdressed.

He caught her in another astonishing kiss, then leaned back. "Get undressed," he said. "I'll be right back."

The bed felt instantly cold as he left her there, and once she realized he was going into the bathroom, she hurriedly wiggled out of her pants and panties. The rush was so she could get out of her really ugly socks. They were made to wear with pants, but to the untrained eye they looked like old-lady stockings. She wanted so badly to be appealing to him, to not spoil it by doing one of a hundred things she'd fretted about in the past. And, no, it didn't matter at all that it was too dark for him to see.

With Graydon, she'd worried about looking fat, about making bodily function sounds even though she knew they were perfectly natural. She'd worried about not being tight enough, about being too tight. She had never quite pleased him, although he wouldn't tell her what it was that made him want to get up after he'd come to watch TV on the couch. He would always fall asleep in the living room, leaving her to wonder.

At least she'd always come. A lot of times she'd had to take care of that for herself, but for an overall selfish man, Graydon had stepped up to the plate his fair share. It still bothered her that they'd stayed together for so long, for all the wrong reasons. Thank goodness he'd found another heiress, someone who matched his family's net worth. They had broken up with a handshake and no regrets. Well, he'd had none. She'd felt as if she'd wasted the only good years she ever had. So soon after college she'd turned recluse, and that had been the end of a traditional sex life for her. But she was quite certain that being alone was far better than being with someone like Graydon. Of course, being with Michael was best of all.

She hoped.

The bed dipped with his return, and she cursed her bad luck for not watching him. She'd like to see him naked, all of him, standing in good light. She'd pictured him so many times; she wondered if she'd gotten any of it right.

He held up a box. "Condoms."

"That makes sense, considering the clothes I found in the drawers."

He got close, his body chilled from his brief foray out. It felt delicious as he pressed up against her. One thing for sure—the trip hadn't dampened his enthusiasm one bit.

"You feel good," he said, his fingers brushing her hair back from her face.

"So do you."

"I've thought about this a lot," he said. "Imagined this a hundred times."

She raised her head, checking his face for lies. "Really?"

"Really."

"I had no idea."

"You weren't meant to. It wouldn't have been appropriate."

She sighed as she settled against him, resting her head on his pillow. "I suppose all bets are off now."

"Yep," he said. "Until I've got you home, this is a whole new ball game. I want you to tell me if anything is uncomfortable or frightening. Aside from the obvious, of course."

"I will."

He touched her chin and made eye contact. "Anything. That means you get to say stop anytime. You can change your mind, and it'll be just fine. Got that?"

She nodded.

"Seriously."

"Michael?"

"Yeah?"

"I appreciate it, but I'm in."

He studied her for a long moment. "Thank God."

She laughed, but his kiss silenced her. Soon his hands were exploring all her private places, touching her with a fascinating mixture of reverence and greed.

Since she'd always been a fan of quid pro quo, she decided to throw caution to the wind and discover

Michael to her heart's content. She wasn't satisfied simply to stroke his cock. She cupped his balls. Delighted at his response, she pinched his delectable ass.

"Hey!"

"Shh," she said before she kissed him again, thrusting her tongue inside him. That quieted him down. Except for his moans, which did strange and wonderful things to her insides.

Nothing she'd felt prepared her, though, for the sensation of his fingers parting her lips, rubbing her all the way up and down, then sliding into her once, twice. Her muscles tightened and her heart beat faster, but there was no panic now. Nothing but excitement and anticipation as his finger found her clit.

He was tender there, the tip of his finger moving in tiny circles, but it still made her eyelids flutter closed, made her abandon his mouth for her own soft, "Oh."

"You like that?" he whispered.

"Mmm," she mumbled, moving her hips to the rhythm of his rubbing.

"You're so wet and hot." He plunged into her again, this time not so gently.

She eased her left leg over his hip, giving him permission to plunder away.

"You're making me crazy."

She smiled. "Me? I'm not the one with the wicked fingers."

"I was going to ask you about that," he said. "I've always imagined you being very, very wicked."

"Me?"

"Oh, yes. Don't forget, I know what you read. What you think is funny. You're not normal, Tate."

"What?"

"I said you're not normal."

"I don't know…." she said. "Should I be insulted?"

"God, no. I love that on the outside you're so prim and together. They all think you're sweet, don't they? They all assume you live so quietly because you're just a good girl who does what she's supposed to."

"I am."

"Yes. But I was there for the discussion of *The Story of O,* remember? I know exactly how you felt about that one scene in *The Big Easy.* You may have been on the phone with Sara, but you were talking to me."

"Oh, God," she said, burying her head in the pillow so he couldn't see her blush. "Was I that obvious?"

"I can't hear you when you mumble into the pillow."

She lifted her head and repeated the question.

"Yes. You were."

She groaned, and this time it wasn't from his busy digits.

"Hey, I liked it."

She shook her head, not wanting to hear his excuses. She knew he was just being polite, and that killed her.

He leaned down so his mouth was close to her ear. "I used to go home and stroke myself to the memory of your voice."

A shiver raced down her spine, and she ended up squeezing his finger quite tightly.

"See? You do like to tease. And you can't tell me you didn't know the effect it had on me. There were all those times when I stood behind the limo door after letting you out. I can't believe you didn't know why."

Looking up once more, she tried to figure out if he was playing her. Was it all just a way to make her forget that she probably wasn't going to live to have sex again? He looked sincere, but that didn't mean a thing. The only real proof she had—if she could call it that—was his very hard dick. Of course, he might be getting off for any number of reasons, only one of them being that he truly wanted her.

"What are you thinking?"

"That this could all be some ploy to distract me."

"It's not. But if it was…?"

She smiled. "Good point. Distract away."

His fingers stilled, his body tensed and the way he looked at her gave her gooseflesh. "Know this, Tate Baxter. I think you're an amazing woman and I'd never do anything to hurt you. Got that?"

She blinked back sudden tears, but he didn't see because he was kissing her again. When he pushed her to her back, she went eagerly, spreading her legs for him. It had been a long time, but she was so ready that when he pushed inside her, she nearly passed out from the pleasure.

While he was in her, fully in her, he somehow lifted her butt and shoved a pillow underneath. So when he moved the next time, he not only filled her perfectly but he rubbed her already engorged clit.

She'd read about this neat little trick but always assumed it was fiction. Boy, was she glad to be wrong.

It was her last coherent thought as Michael proceeded to rock not just her world but all the worlds in the galaxy.

She came like a Roman candle, and he had to kiss her so she wouldn't wake everyone on the East Coast.

Flushed, gasping, eyes closed, she felt him remove the pillow from under her butt, then pull the covers up to her chest. She wasn't sure if his gentle kiss on the forehead was real or a dream or both.

HE GOT OUT OF THE bed and went straight for the bathroom so his moaning wouldn't wake her.

He pulled off the damn rubber, then turned on the cold water, whispering every curse in every language he knew. He'd held off before, but damn, it had never hurt like this. He was getting old, that's all. Old and unable to control himself as well.

It seemed to take forever for his dick to calm the hell down, and even then getting dressed made him swear again. He'd done his job, all right. She'd fallen asleep, as predicted. Now all he had to do was make sure she didn't wake up in the middle of his escape.

He got his comb out of his back pocket. No one ever thought to take the comb. Not only was it good for handcuffs, he could open one hell of a lot of locks with this puppy. It was cheap, too. He'd bought a pack of fifty for five bucks.

He slipped the scissors into his pocket, then turned off the light. He'd get himself into the saloon, praying no one was watching the door. All he'd need was a few seconds of good surveillance and he could go on the offensive.

He stepped out of the head to find Tate still sleeping. Then he turned off the cabin light and made sure there was no bleed of light around the door. It was dark, which was just what he needed.

He quietly made his way to the door, which only took him a minute to unlock. Then he was in the saloon and he closed the door behind him.

Martini wasn't sitting in his big leather chair anymore. Charlie had fallen asleep on the couch, and Jazz had drifted off with his head on the side counter.

He made his way toward Jazz, determined to get his gun before taking him out, just in case. As he reached for the weapon, pain tore through him like lightning. Then black.

# 10

TATE TOUCHED MICHAEL'S shoulder, really worried now that the hit on the head had done serious damage. He'd been out for hours, and the swelling, despite the damp cloths she'd kept on it, was bad.

Just after he'd been dumped on the bed, the boat had pulled anchor and set out. She had no idea if they were going to the Cayman Islands or simply out to sea to dispose of bodies, but she did know they were traveling fast. When she'd looked out the porthole, she'd seen no land at all in the early-morning light.

If only he'd wake up.

She sat back on the bed watching his chest rise and fall. He'd been so wonderful to her last night. It had changed everything for her about sex, and if this hadn't been the single worst experience of her life, she'd have been in heaven.

More then ever she wanted to survive this. Not just to get over her fears but to see what would happen between her and Michael. Was she the worst person on Earth to be thinking of their future together while he might be seriously hurt? She supposed it was no worse than her prognosis. They'd either die tonight, in the cold depths of the sea, or in about a week, after she'd signed her money away. Or Michael would recover and he'd save her.

She decided right then to focus on option three.

Her father wouldn't have hired him if he wasn't the best, right? And he'd gotten them this far. Okay, so his escape plan last night hadn't gone so well. But, come on, the guy had had no way of knowing what was behind the door. At least he'd tried.

Things would get trickier now, though. Assuming they were heading for the Cayman's, they'd have to get fuel. She wasn't sure how often they'd have to stop, but when they did, there would be a chance.

She looked at his face, at his very dark, long eyelashes. At his lips, perfect for a man. His nose was pretty damn nice, too. Oh, who was she kidding? He was a babe, and even her, with her limited knowledge about men, knew he'd been around the block many, many times. Probably with fabulous women, because, well, come on.

Had he really told her the truth last night?

She shivered remembering his whispered words just before he'd made love to her. God, that was the sexiest thing ever. She sighed, knowing she was behaving like an adolescent.

And why not? She'd stunted her growth, her heart had atrophied—and for what? All that planning, all that fear hadn't helped one damn bit. She'd still been kidnapped. So she could have been having a fabulous life all this time instead of whining about her regrets.

At least she wouldn't regret last night. If she had to go, this was the way to do it. Well, not *this*. This sucked. She needed Michael to be okay. She could face whatever came next if he was beside her. Alone? She'd rather die than be that scared again.

A moan made her freeze, hold her breath. She watched him, afraid to blink, as he moaned again, moved his head. He winced, and that had to be a good sign, right?

"Michael?"

He opened his eyes just a little, then closed them again. "What happened?" His voice sounded thick, dry.

"They hit you."

"With what? A refrigerator?"

"I don't know. They brought you in last night. Well, early this morning, although I'm not sure what time. They dumped you on the bed and told me to tell you that if you tried that again, they wouldn't be so nice."

He tried to lift his head but just winced again. "Yeah, they were real swell."

"It was brave of you to try," she said. "Hold on. I'll cool down the washcloth." She took the small blue towel from behind his head, making him hiss, then hurried to the bathroom. The water was really cold, which was good. She wished she had ice, though.

When she got back to the bed she saw he hadn't moved at all. She tried to be gentle as she applied the cold compress, but she hurt him anyway.

"Is it me or are we moving?"

"We set off sometime around sunrise. I think."

"Right." He put his hand on the back of his head, trying to feel the extent of the damage, but in the end he just held the cloth and slowly sat up. "Jesus."

She reached over beside the bed and brought back

a glass of water and a bottle of aspirin. "I got this ready. I figured—"

He moaned again and took the aspirin bottle from her hand. He brought the cap up to his mouth and snapped the bottle open with his teeth. Then he dumped a bunch of the small white pills in his mouth. At least six.

"Won't that—"

He dropped the open bottle, took the glass and drained it in a few hard gulps.

"That's a lot of aspirin," she said.

"It's a very large headache."

"You need to eat something, then. Your stomach lining will get very irritated."

He looked at her through shuttered eyes. "I appreciate the concern, but my stomach lining is the least of our worries."

"Fine."

He patted her hand. "Don't be hurt. It's good of you to care. But I've taken this many before and I've been okay."

"Still…"

"You're right. I hope they feed us soon. I promise to eat every bite."

She sat back, adjusting some of the pillows so she could look at him comfortably. "How did you get into the other room? I didn't even see you go."

"You were sleeping."

"I gathered."

"I'm pretty good with locks."

"I gathered that, too. But we have no idea how many people there are on board. It would have been pure luck if you'd been successful."

He winced again, and she was pretty sure it wasn't about the pain in his head.

"I'm sorry," he said. "I shouldn't have let things get this far."

"You've done everything you could."

"Not everything."

"What do you mean?"

"Nothing. I'll figure this out. I won't let them hurt you."

She reached over and touched his hand. "I know."

He looked away, and she wished she'd never brought up the subject. "Let me get you some more water."

"It's okay. I'll go."

"No, you're—"

"I want to wash up," he said. "And you should go through those clothes again. I'm pretty sure I saw at least one T-shirt that would fit you."

"I don't know…."

"Try. A shower will make you feel better."

She smiled at him, amazed that even now he was thinking of her. That he could look so good even when he was in so much pain.

Once he'd closed the bathroom door, she went to the dresser and found a couple of men's T-shirts that she thought they could each wear. There was also a bikini that would substitute for underwear. She'd wash her own in the shower, then…

Would she be alive tomorrow to put on her own underpants? Did she want to die wearing someone else's skimpy bikini?

Tears welled at the thought of never seeing her father again. He'd overprotected her, but he'd done it out of love. For all his preoccupation with business, he'd always kept her close. Loved her the best way he knew how.

And, oh, God, never to see Sara again? That hurt as deeply as the thoughts of her father. Sara might not be a blood relative, but in every way that mattered she was a sister. A damn good one, too. They hardly ever fought, but she never hesitated to tell Tate the unvarnished truth.

The ache to see her friend again took her breath away, and she sat down on the edge of the bed. It was probably a good thing Dr. Bay wasn't around. What an idiot. Fake kidnappings. Please. The woman needed major therapy herself.

Tate sniffed, her anger at her therapist distracting her from the pain of her losses. Once again she thanked God for Michael. She'd have lost it without him. She just wished she could do something to make him feel better.

AT LEAST, MICHAEL thought, there was no way he could feel worse. What the hell had happened to him? He was supposed to be a goddamn warrior, a fighter, a champion.

As the water poured down over him in the small shower, he couldn't think of one thing that had gone right in the last two days. Even the good parts made him feel like shit. Tate was going to find out about Charlie. She was. And he had to be the one to tell her. Only…how? Especially now, when he didn't have a plan other than to wait and strike at the next opportunity.

He'd be lucky if she didn't strike him first.

He didn't even know who'd hit him. Or with what. Or how many people were currently on board. Or what direction they were going.

Maybe it was just his turn. Charlie'd been the bad-luck magnet all these years. Maybe now it would come up roses for his brother while Michael went straight down the tubes.

He grabbed the soap and scrubbed up, shaking off his self-pity and thinking about how he was going to tell her. It seemed so naive, from this vantage point, to think his problems could have been solved by sexing her to sleep. Talk about stupid. Talk about thinking with his dick.

He moaned as he fell forward, then groaned when he actually hit his sore head against the fiberglass wall. He should go into that saloon and fight until he couldn't fight anymore. With luck, he'd wipe them all out before he flung himself overboard to be eaten by sharks. Then Tate could radio for help. The end.

She'd still find out Charlie was his brother, but he'd have died bravely trying to save her, so that would prove that he hadn't been…

"Shit." He sighed deeply, closed his eyes and turned the shower to dead cold.

ED MARTINI FINISHED his eggs Benedict while he watched the final race at Santa Anita. He wasn't even thinking about the money he'd just made from the race or the five million stashed in his safe back at the house. He was thinking about fifty million tax-free dollars. The dough wouldn't make a big difference in his life. Hell, he did everything he wanted now. But he'd know, goddammit, he'd know each and every day that he had fifty million fucking dollars that Sheila wouldn't be able to touch. Not even with those god-awful two-inch fingernails of hers. What the woman wanted with little palm trees painted in green on her fingers was beyond him. They looked like crap, but he supposed they went along with her bleached hair and her wide-load ass.

The trick would be to let her think he had the money. She couldn't be sure, because if she was sure, she'd sic the IRS on him. But she had to think he had it and he wasn't giving it to her. That would make her insane. More than any new girlfriend, even one who was twenty-five. More than any new car. It would kill Sheila that he had that much cash that she couldn't spend. The bitch.

"Hey, boss?"

"Yeah, Jazz?"

"I never been to the Cayman Islands. They nice?"

"Yeah."

"Nice women?"

"Oh, yeah."

"How long is it gonna take us to get there?"

"This boat? If we hit good weather? Maybe eight days."

"Fuck. What are we gonna do for eight days?"

Ed leaned back in his chair. He knew just what he was gonna do: conduct his business, like usual. Just 'cause he wasn't in town didn't mean he wasn't raking it in. "Jazz, you just concentrate on keeping your eye on our happy couple. You caught him last night, but he still managed to get out of that locked room."

"It won't happen again."

"Be sure it doesn't."

Jazz, who had eaten his bacon and eggs in about ten seconds, then cleaned his gun, lowered his voice. "What about him?" he said, nodding toward Charlie.

"Charlie," Ed said.

The kid stopped eating, nearly choking on his bacon. "Yeah, boss?"

"You finish your breakfast, then take food in to your brother and his girlfriend. You make sure he understands that if he tries anything like he did last night, it won't be good for your health."

Charlie swallowed again. "Okay, sure. He won't do it again. I swear to God. He won't. He promised my old—"

"I don't care. Just make sure he understands."

Charlie nodded unhappily as he pushed his plate away.

THE SHOWER WAS SO small she kept bumping her elbows. Hers at home was quite large, with three different showerheads. It doubled as a steam room, and she could also simulate the patter of a rain-forest squall if she so desired. Here, the water was marginally warm, the soap was blue and smelled like antiseptic. And she didn't trust for a moment that one of those men from the saloon wouldn't burst through the door.

Yes, she still had faith that Michael would stop anything bad from happening, but she'd discovered early on that logic had little to do with irrational fears. Hence the word *irrational*.

She kept washing, wondering what her hair was

going to look like after using that dime-store mousse she'd found. What her skin would feel like after a few days away from her Intensité Volumizing Serum. Oh, well. She'd make do. What choice did she have?

Without even reading the label, she washed her hair, then put conditioner on, and as she rinsed she wished she'd brought the darn razor in with her. Although she wouldn't have been able to shave her legs, not in this small space. So she'd do it after. She could still rinse off in the shower.

She thought about Michael for the hundredth time since she'd climbed in the shower. He'd smelled awfully good after his. But then, he was a man. Oh, was he ever.

She laughed at herself, wondering if she was going to be this moony teen the whole way to the Caymans. It wouldn't matter, she supposed. No one would know. And why shouldn't she do exactly as she pleased?

Most people thought she did, anyway. She knew they didn't dare compare her to Paris Hilton, but there were other trust-fund babies that were around her age. She'd heard them talk about how ridiculous she looked in her old-fashioned limo, how she dressed like Queen Elizabeth. She wasn't completely protected from the gossip and the backbiting.

How many nights had she wept herself to sleep watching those awful newsmagazine shows? She hadn't really wanted to shock the world. Well, mostly. But she had wanted to make some kind of splash, even a little one.

The charities didn't count. Anyone could do her job. Anyone with the right connections. It was easy to give money away when you had her father's strict guidelines to follow.

But she'd never been to a big premiere or an opening night on Broadway. She'd never been to any of the clubs or found herself searching for a predawn breakfast after carousing all night.

She didn't just dress like Queen Elizabeth, she partied like her, too.

Tate turned abruptly, tired of her pity party. She turned off the water and stepped out onto the blue fluffy towel. As she dried off she promised herself that she wouldn't go to that place again. If she had to dwell on the past, it would be to remember all those self-defense classes, her weapons training.

There was no reason she shouldn't stand shoulder to shoulder with Michael. Fight no matter what.

She grabbed the tiny bikini and put the sucker on. It was tight. And, jeez, her boobs looked huge. But that was okay. So was the T-shirt. Also tight but not too horrible.

She'd also dug out a pair of shorts—men's, but they were a size medium, and if she tied the little waistband inside, they wouldn't fall down.

Dammit. She'd forgotten to shave. She rubbed her leg, and it wasn't so bad. Tomorrow, though, for sure. For now, she put on the mousse and combed her hair. She debated a moment about using the hair dryer, but it would probably be better if she let it dry naturally.

Then she looked at the makeup that had been left in the bathroom. It was no use. She couldn't use some other woman's makeup. Not for anything. It was as bad as sharing a toothbrush.

So she washed her panties and her bra, and as she

went to hang them in the shower she heard shouting just outside the bathroom door.

Immediately her heart started pounding as though she was seconds from an attack. When she turned to the door, the tunnel vision started, taking her straight down the road to immobility and failure.

She closed her eyes. Took several deep breaths. She pictured her safe place, but the vision of her waterfall didn't help. The voices—Michael's and another man's—were too loud.

Then she changed her visualization. It wasn't her old green meadow. It was Michael. His face. His eyes. The way he looked at her, then smiled.

She smelled his skin and remembered his taste. Salty, sexy. She brought up the memory of his fingers on her face, and then his fingers weren't near her face. He was leaning over her, and his intentions were incredibly clear.

He wanted her. He wanted *her.*

The vision changed once more, and she was carrying her Sig Sauer. And there was Michael. Tall, handsome as sin. And he had his gun, too. He had her back. And she had his. No one was getting past the two of them.

She went to the bathroom door, and as she swung it open she heard the other one yelling.

"You swore to him, Mikey! You swore to our father that you'd take care of me. You think breaking in to hurt Mr. Martini is keeping me safe? You got to cool it, Mikey, or he's gonna kill all of us, okay?"

Tate's vision narrowed once more. All she could see was the look on Michael's face. Shock, anger. Guilt.

*He was in on this. He was in on this. She'd slept with him, and he was in on it.*

# *11*

MICHAEL SHOT A LOOK at Charlie that had him scrambling out the door, but his main concern was Tate. She looked unsteady, panicked. Everything he'd hoped to avoid.

He went to the bathroom door and put his arm gently around her waist. It was a testament to how bad off she was that she didn't slap him in the face. "Come on. Let's get you to the bed."

She struggled, but so faintly he figured he'd better get her to lie down before she fell down. Goddamn Charlie. It wasn't enough to fuck up his own life, he had to fuck up Tate's. Good job, asshole.

As he took her to the bed, he reached for her wrist and got a feel for her pulse. Dammit, it was off the charts, a full-blown panic attack, and he wasn't at all sure he could help her.

He turned her around and pressed gently on her shoulders. She sat, her hands limp by her sides, her face pale and lifeless. The only thing animated about her was her breathing. She took great gulps, as if the oxygen was far too weak to sustain her.

He wished he could enjoy her shorts, her tight little T-shirt, but he gave them only a glance as he tried to gauge his next move. He needed her to understand what was going on. He expected no forgiveness at all, but he did think they could work together until this horror show was over. If he could just get her to hear him—to believe him.

He sat down next to her, his shoulder touching hers. She didn't move, but she didn't lean into him either. "Tate, I need you to listen to me. First, this is all my fault. However, it wasn't intentional. My brother has been a pain in my ass for a long, long time. I should have cut it off between us years ago, but...

"Anyway, he came to my place, and when I had to leave the room, he broke into my safe. He saw the information I had on Brody. I wouldn't give him the money to pay off his bookie, so he stole that information and used it as a way of getting out of debt. That's why you're here—because I let Charlie into my apartment. I didn't realize he'd go this far—and I should have."

As he paused he saw her eyes jig over to look at him, but they went back to staring straight ahead a second later. "I know it's hard to believe anyone could be stupid enough to let Charlie in the same borough, let alone his apartment. He's been nothing but trouble from the time he was a kid. He stole, he took drugs, he had no sense about the world. It was always someone else's fault with Charlie, mostly mine.

"My mother had died a long time ago, and my father did his best to keep Charlie out of trouble. He got sick—my dad, I mean—and he made me promise I'd take care of Charlie. I gave him my word, and that's not something I take lightly.

"It was all right because I spent so much time overseas. You know I was in intelligence work, but you don't know why I left the service. It was Charlie, one more time. He stole a briefcase from a fellow officer's car. He was caught and he went to jail, but because of me they didn't charge him with treason. I couldn't stay in the service after that."

He wasn't sure, but he thought she'd leaned a little more his way. Hell, he wasn't even sure if she was listening or, if she was, whether she believed any part of his story. The only concrete change he saw was that she wasn't struggling quite so hard to breathe.

"You feeling a little better? I can get you some water."

She shook her head, and he wondered if she was saying no to the water or to feeling better.

"Is there anything I can do?"

"Why should I believe you?" Her voice was low, a monotone of bleak expectation.

"There's no reason at all. I had planned on telling you about Charlie, but honestly I wasn't sure when. I didn't expect you to have a minute of sympathy for my situation, but I didn't want you to hate me so much that you wouldn't accept my help."

"You made love to me."

"Oh, God. That's what I was most afraid of. I didn't have ulterior motives—no, that's not true. There was a hope that, after, you could get some rest. But the motivation for kissing you, that's been around for a long time. I'm not sorry we did it, only that I wasn't smart enough to know the best way to handle this situation. You've been doing so great. Your attacks have been less frequent and less severe, and if you can keep that up until we're safe, then it'll change your life."

"When did you know?"

"That Charlie was behind this?"

She nodded.

"When I followed you here. When I looked into the saloon I saw him. A few seconds later I was knocked out."

She turned her head to look at him. At least she had a little more color. "The fifty million, heading off for the Caymans…it's too much to believe."

He nodded. "I know some things about Ed Martini. There's a reason we're on this boat. Once he'd gotten the ransom from your father…"

"He'd have killed me."

Michael nodded.

"I imagine he'll kill me after I sign the papers at the bank. The question is, will he kill you?"

"He won't kill either of us. I told him about the bank to stall for time. I had to make the prize big enough, so I told him fifty million. I had to make it far enough away that he'd have to take on fuel and supplies."

"They knocked you out last night when they should have killed you."

"Because they think I'm the only one who can get you to sign the papers."

She shook her head a little, and her eyes welled with tears. "You tell a good story, Michael. But then, that was your job, wasn't it? Telling stories to manipulate people?"

"That's right."

"So how can I know? How can I possibly believe what you've told me?"

"I don't know. I do know that I'm going to resign as soon as I have you back safely."

"I wish I hadn't heard him," she said. "It was so much better."

"You would have found out. It was inevitable. Ironically, I'd planned on telling you right after your shower."

"Michael," she said, whispering, "why does it bother me more that you made love to me than that you had me kidnapped?"

He wiped his face with his hand, wishing like hell he could tell her at least one thing that would convince her that he wasn't lying. "It's because you doubt yourself. How attractive you are. How smart and funny."

"Oh, don't. Don't do that to me. It's hard enough."

"Is there anything I could say that would help?"

"I know that I can't trust anything you've said or will say. I might have a panic disorder, but I've been well trained about con men. I've got that fifty million. And my father, he's got so much more."

Her color was back and her cheeks looked flushed. She wasn't gasping for breath any longer. Her panic had diminished as her anger had grown, which was good. She needed to be angry.

"I imagine you've seen your share of gigolos."

"Some of the best. That's why—"

"Why what?"

"I can't have this conversation." She stood up and took a deep breath. "I can't be in this room with you."

He was the breathless one now. Why had he thought the truth would be enough? It rarely was, and if he were Tate, he wouldn't have bought it, either. He just hadn't realized how much he'd wanted a miracle. "I understand." He looked up at her. "Unfortunately there's nowhere for me to go."

She looked behind her, at the door. "You can go be with your brother."

"Uh, no. Martini already let me know that if I didn't get you to sign the papers, he'd kill Charlie first."

"Why should I care?"

"Because he said he'd kill you second."

SARA WAS GOING TO lose it. They'd heard nothing, absolutely nothing, and William had delivered the ransom hours and hours ago.

She'd paced all six thousand square feet of Tate's place. She'd tried to comfort William, but he was inconsolable. Believed his daughter was dead. Believed Michael had been behind the kidnapping. There were security people all over the place, all his phones had been forwarded to Tate's main line. And they'd heard nothing, not a word.

What concerned her most was William having a heart attack. She'd called his personal physician to be here until this was resolved, and the doctor should be arriving any minute. She went to the fridge again and took out a head of lettuce. It wasn't her usual kind of snack, but it was here and she had to stuff something in her mouth. She broke the lettuce up into chunks and put it in a colander to drain.

"Is there something I can make you?"

Sara jumped at Pilar's voice. "No, thank you. If I have a bite of something decent, I'll never stop. I'm going to chew lettuce."

"I can fix a quick vinaigrette—"

"Thanks, Pilar, but I wasn't kidding. I will never stop."

"I understand. Food is oddly comforting."

"Maybe you can fix something for Mr. Baxter."

"He's refused me several times."

"You know, I think if you put a platter near him with bite-size treats, he'll end up taking one, and that will lead to more."

Pilar nodded. "I'll do that. I've got twenty minutes until I have to take the casserole out for the staff."

Sara sighed as she took the lettuce from under the running water. She let it drip, thinking about how incredible Pilar's casseroles were, and put a chunk of the not-quite salad into her mouth. It tasted about as good as she'd expected.

"Michael didn't do this," Pilar said.

"I know."

"Mr. Baxter doesn't."

"He needs someone to blame. This family has a history with kidnappings."

Pilar went to the fridge and pulled out an array of goodies. She set up on one of the huge counters and started to prepare delectable treats without a glance at a cookbook. Huge fresh figs were sliced down the middle, then stuffed with a wedge of Gorgonzola cheese. Just looking at them made Sara feel way too sorry for herself.

It was the doorbell that saved her, and she hurried out, all thoughts of figs buried beneath her prayers. Unfortunately it was the doctor, not Tate.

The doctor. She made sure he sat with William, and despite the older man's objections, he started an immediate checkup. "William, I'll be back," she said.

"Where are you going?"

"To pay someone a visit."

He looked at her, concerned.

"Don't worry. I'll be fine. It won't take me long. I'll be back before you can blink."

"Please."

She strode toward the elevator, knowing this had to be done and knowing she was the right person to do it.

MICHAEL WAS RIGHT—there was nowhere for him to go. But she needed some time to think without looking at him. The only place was the head. She'd been so positive in there, what, fifteen minutes ago? Maybe she could find something to hang on to in there.

Without a word, she went back to the head and closed the door. It looked smaller, uglier. It didn't matter because Michael wasn't here.

Michael wasn't there, either. Not the Michael she thought she knew. What was she supposed to believe? Everything had come together so easily. They had to have been aware of Elizabeth or they wouldn't have put her out of commission so easily. They'd known exactly where she'd be. How, if Michael hadn't told them?

She sat down on the toilet and willed herself— uselessly, it turned out—not to cry. The tears were heavy and hot, and her chest hurt as if she'd been kicked by a mule.

He'd set her up. There was no other conclusion she could come to, right? He'd been dismissed from the one job he'd loved and been forced to become a baby-sitter. It had to be humiliating. It only made sense to want revenge, and since he couldn't get back at the

Army, he could get even with her. The stupid rich chick who was a perfect mark. She was already crazy, it wouldn't take much to immobilize her. Persuade her that he was on her side. That he would be her salvation. Of course she'd sign over her money if it meant saving her life, but it didn't, did it? She would never be released. He would sneak about the boat, but he wouldn't be successful because that wasn't the plan. All he had to do was have her believe in him. Have her need him again.

The real tragedy? She wanted to. Desperately.

Last night had been incredible. Not just the sex but the fact that she hadn't spent every single second trapped in a panic attack. She'd slept. She hadn't had a nightmare.

It was better than anything she'd ever anticipated, better than she'd been even in imaginary scenarios.

More than that, Michael had been the safest of her safe places. She remembered the feelings that had coursed through her body as she'd pictured him in her mind. He'd been right there with her, but she'd never seen him more clearly than with her eyes closed.

Her heart was beating hard even now, just thinking about it. She'd liked him so much. Those talks in the car—those couldn't have been faked. Wasn't possible. He'd never known what they were going to talk about. He didn't know what books she'd read, what movies she'd seen. So his reactions had been real. Honest.

God, what if he was telling her the truth?

She unrolled some tissue and blew her nose, then got some more and wiped her eyes. She wished she could talk to Sara. Sara would know. Sara would tell her the truth and she'd completely look out for her. Unlike Dr. Bay.

SARA FELT AMAZINGLY calm as she read the new issue of *Vanity Fair*. She'd never get tired of seeing George Clooney as the cover subject. Not ever. She'd seen him in person three times, and he was the single dreamiest man on earth. And, yes, she'd seen Mr. Pitt in person, too. Of course, if forced, she'd also go out with Brad, but her first choice would be George.

The door opened and Sara stood up. She'd had to wait longer than she'd hoped, but it was worth it. Or it would be in another minute.

She approached a well dressed woman. Very well-dressed. Her short, dark bob was perfect and so was her makeup. She lived the life, here on Park Avenue. "Dr. Bay? I'm Tate's friend, Sara."

She nodded. "Has there been any word?"

"No. None."

"Oh, my God."

"I do have one thing to tell you."

"If I can be of any help, of course I will."

"I think you've been about as helpful as you're going to get."

"Pardon me?"

"There is no pardon for you. What kind of moron takes a girl who's been absolutely traumatized by her own kidnapping and the death of her best friend and suggests she stage her own kidnapping? I mean, of all the idiotic, irresponsible—"

"Now you just wait a minute. I don't know who you

think you are, but my suggestions to my patient were completely legitimate and not in the least irresponsible."

"What are you, insane? She's been kidnapped. For real. And it's entirely possible she won't be coming back. Which will only mean one thing—they've killed her. You understand what she went through? Her worst fear in the world, and she had to live through it. She had to know she was going to die." Sara wiped the tears from her face with the heel of her hand. "If Michael wasn't with her..."

"I'm very sorry for what's happened to Tate, but you must know that I bear no responsibility. This was purely a coincidence, a tragic one, but it had nothing to do—"

"Don't you dare. Don't you—" Sara turned, fury so great inside her that she thought she might burst or go crazy or... She pulled back, and when she swung it was with all her weight behind her. The crack was loud and the pain shot up her arm and hurt like the devil. But Dr. Bay, who wasn't responsible, who had nothing to do with anything, had gone flying back into her pristine office with the fresh flowers and the expensive furniture. Her hand was on her cheek and she was crying. Finally.

"You're just lucky it was me who came after you. If it had been Michael, you'd be dead."

HE SAT ON THE BED, waiting. Remembering when he was a kid, when Charlie was really young and his mom was still alive. Charlie hadn't been a screwup then. He'd just been a little kid, like every other little kid, and he'd been Michael's responsibility, even back then. When anything went wrong with Charlie, his mother had given him this real disappointed look.

He still saw that look. Felt it. As fucked up as Charlie was, Michael was still responsible. Even now. With Tate in the bathroom. With Tate believing the worst. Still, the idea of walking into the saloon and shooting Charlie made him sick.

What if it came down to that? To choosing between Tate and Charlie? What then?

His first responsibility was to Tate. That was a fact and nothing would change it. He just didn't like the idea of Charlie dying. Not because the stupid son of a bitch didn't deserve it, but Michael had a deathbed promise hanging over his head, and even though he knew it was superstitious nonsense, it didn't feel that way.

Charlie had crossed the line. If there was a way to save him, then Michael would—as long as it didn't endanger Tate. If not, well, then he'd tell his father he was sorry when he joined him in hell.

Decision made, he went back to waiting. Worrying. Wishing. It wasn't like him. He didn't wish for the impossible. He never had. But when it came to Tate, he did a lot of things he'd never done before.

# _12_

AFTER AN EXCRUCIATING night of no sleep, of remembering what it had been like to make love to him, of reliving the moment of betrayal over and over, Tate finally slept as the sky began to soften into day.

She woke, startled at the sound of the door slamming shut. There was Michael in his borrowed T-shirt and his chauffeur's pants, holding a tray with food and coffee. At the sight, her stomach clenched, and she knew she wouldn't be eating much. Of course, it didn't matter, did it? Nothing did. She would die soon and this torment would be over. That's all she wanted. In fact, maybe there was a way to speed things up. She'd have to think about that.

Michael put the tray on the dresser and turned to her. She wasted no time in slipping out of the bed. She no longer cared about the clean clothes problem or shaving her legs.

"Tate, we need to—"

She slammed the bathroom door closed behind her. By the time she'd washed her face, brushed her teeth and her hair, she'd realized she couldn't go out there. He would end up convincing her that he'd had her best interest at heart. That he wasn't a thief, that he'd made love to her because he'd been attracted, or in love or some other fairy tale.

At least she could sit down. Of course, the john wasn't exactly her idea of a great chair, but it was better than looking at him. Her real shame wasn't that she'd been deceived but, that knowing she'd been deceived, she still wanted him.

That's what made her sick. That's what terrified her.

How could she want so badly to believe him? Why did she have to force herself out of the fantasy where they lived happily ever after? She truly did need a shrink. Not Dr. Bay, of course, but a good shrink.

She laughed as her chin dropped to her chest. Too late for shrinkage now. She wondered if they'd kill her first before they threw her in the water. That's something she'd beg for, if she had to. The thought of drowning…

"Tate?" Michael's voice came from directly outside the door. "Do you want some coffee? I can hand you a cup. You don't have to come out."

"No." She waited, but he didn't respond. She wished there was a peephole. It would have been so much better if she could know where he was.

She stood, whipped off her clothes and got under the shower, not taking the soap or the shampoo; she was there for the water. She'd always had her best ideas in the shower, and now would be a really good time for something brilliant to occur.

She laughed, inhaling water, then choking for a long, long time. Which was when she had the thought. She wasn't sure it was brilliant—in fact, it was probably an excellent example of how she'd lost her mind—but there it was. And there it stayed. All day.

MICHAEL GLANCED OUT the porthole, not surprised to see the red sky of sunset. He hadn't taken a drink or eaten a bite because he really hadn't wanted to bother Tate in the bathroom, but things were getting a bit hairy.

His personal problem wasn't nearly as worrisome as what Tate was going through. He hated that he'd put her in this position, but he couldn't figure out what to say to make things better. He'd told her the truth and he feared that anything else would sever any slight hope that she could believe him. But the truth seemed meager and foolish. Perhaps if he had told her the moment he'd been shoved inside the cabin, she'd have bought it. But he'd been an idiot about that, too.

It was difficult not to put all the blame on Charlie. Granted, Charlie deserved a great deal of it. But then, he did, too. As long as he was able to get an accurate picture of what was real, then he had a chance to save her. If he indulged himself in blaming Charlie, he would lose sight of the objective: keep Tate alive. That was his whole purpose, and he could put nothing ahead of that. His second goal was to keep Tate sane. To help her not be terrified every minute. Right now, that was the more difficult task, but again, if he kept his eye on the prize, he could get—

The head door opened. Tate stood in the doorway, leaning on the jamb, her arms crossed over the boys' T-shirt they'd found in the dresser.

She looked good. Her color was fine. In fact, she seemed a bit flushed. Her chest rose and fell normally. There were no apparent tremors. The only thing that looked off was the puffiness of her eyes, but even that was in the regular range. He wanted to say something, anything, but he held back, afraid that whatever he did say would be wrong and would send her straight back to panic.

"So these are my options," she said, her voice even and considered. "I can do the completely logical, rational thing and not believe one thing you've said. It makes perfect sense that you set me up for this. I mean, who else knew we were going to be at Prada? That Elizabeth wouldn't be able to get to me in that tiny little window of opportunity? It makes sense that you came after me, knowing I had a great deal of money in a secret account. Why else was I taken to a boat? It made getting the money easy and my disposal a snap.

"It also makes sense that you would bring your brother into this. That he'd know someone who had the boat, had the means, had the manpower. Everything points to you. I'm not being melodramatic, either. Any cop on any *Law & Order* would nail your ass before the first commercial."

She straightened, and with arms still crossed, still protective, she took two steps toward him. "Or, against all logic and reason, I can believe you. I can shift my focus to our relationship in the car. How much I enjoyed our long conversations and how much I admired your own logic and reason. I can remember how you made me laugh.

"And I can think about making love with you and how you made me feel. Of course, if I choose to believe you and I find out I was wrong, I will want to die, so that works in your favor. If I'm right, and you're innocent and then you die... Well, you're just not allowed to, okay? Because I am taking a huge, stupid risk here. It makes no sense, and if my father knew, he'd strangle me for my own good."

She walked a little closer to the bed, and when she stood in front of him, telling him in no uncertain terms that she was on his side, she dropped her arms. He looked up at her face. She looked beautiful, with her hair thick and wavy, with no makeup, with no defenses whatsoever.

He stood. "Tate, I can't believe I'm going to say this. Unfortunately I have no choice."

Her face got sad and she bit her lower lip.

"No, it's not like that. Don't fret. But I have to use the toilet." He squeezed her shoulders. "You were in there a really long time."

Desperate now, he dashed the few feet to his objective, kicking the door shut behind him.

Tate stared at the closed door. She smiled despite herself, and a moment later she was laughing, picturing the poor guy crossing his legs as the hours had crawled by. She'd taken advantage of her location a couple of times, but it hadn't occurred to her that he might need to, too.

She sat on the edge of the bed as she laughed, not just at his predicament but at her own willingness to live knee-deep in denial. It was utter nonsense to believe him, and she knew it, but if this was the end, she'd rather go out with the charming liar, thank you. She'd rather have as much sex as was humanly possible. She'd prefer not to have any more panic attacks and to continue to use Michael as her safe place.

Either way, believing him or not, she doubted she

was walking away from this, so what the hell? She'd wasted so much time, so much life, that this seemed the sanest decision she'd made since dumping Graydon.

"So you think that was funny?" Michael had taken her place leaning against the doorjamb. His arms were crossed over his chest, which was too bad. He had a great chest.

"Yes. I think so. Although I do apologize for putting you in that dire circumstance."

He nodded. Kept staring at her.

"Well? Comments? Suggestions?"

His wonderful lips curled up into a great smile. "A couple of comments. No suggestions."

"Go ahead."

"I completely understand not believing a word I said."

"Thanks."

"I thought about laying all my theories on the table, but now that seems irrelevant. This is clearly an act of faith."

"That's true."

"I just want to state what I know about you. These aren't opinions, by the way. They're facts."

"Uh-oh."

His expression grew serious. "Don't jump to conclusions." He came to the bed and sat down next to her. When she looked into his eyes, he looked straight back. "I know you've got strengths that are invisible to you. I know that you haven't been helped to see them by your father or your shrink. I know that Sara's been a damn good friend and that you should listen to her more closely.

"I know that it feels insurmountable, this panic

disorder of yours, but I'm damned impressed by how you've handled yourself since we've been here. By all rights, you should be comatose by now. A drooling mess. But you're not, are you? You've made a very tough decision, and that's not easy for the sanest people out there. You chose life, Tate, and given all the evidence, you shouldn't have."

She turned away from him as the tears threatened to fall. She'd never have guessed he'd use this opportunity to talk about her. To give her the single greatest pep talk of her life. She'd imagined him shoring up his alibi, redirecting her suspicions.

Maybe believing in him wasn't the stupidest decision she'd ever made.

"There's food here, and I know you haven't had any all day."

She sniffed, blinked, then turned to look at the plates. Each one had a sandwich, a few baby carrots and a bag of chips. Suddenly it looked better than a meal at Nobu.

She grabbed one of the plates and tore off the cellophane. Michael laughed and did the same with his plate. For the next ten minutes they did nothing but scarf. He got up once and went to the vanity, where there were two sodas. Even though neither was diet, she took hers eagerly.

The idyll didn't last long.

Michael wiped his mouth with the small paper napkin and put his empty can on the clean plate. "That sucked and was great all at the same time."

She took both plates back to the vanity. "That's also true." As she turned back to him, she was caught completely by surprise by an enormous belch. She felt her cheeks heat as she put her hand to her mouth.

Michael grinned as if he'd just seen Santa.

"I'm glad my humiliation pleases you so much."

"Hey, tit for tat."

"I suppose so," she said. "It's weird not being able to retreat."

"Is that what you want to do?"

"Not right now, but I did about twenty seconds ago."

"You clearly never had a brother."

She shook her head. "I had Lisa. Then Sara. That's it."

"That sounds pretty good to me."

Tate had a rush of anticipation for what the night would hold as she walked back to the bed. She sat next to him and touched his thigh. "There's no Sara in your life?"

"Nope. I had some good friends in the Army. But that's over."

"Are you sure your friends are over? Or are you just embarrassed?"

"I'm sure. *They're* embarrassed, and that doesn't tend to work with us military types. It's easiest for everyone if I stay under the radar."

"I hope you make more friends after this is over. Without Sara…"

"Hey," he said. "Sara."

"You can't have her. She's mine."

"Oh."

"Not that way. Jeez, are all men so predictable?"

"Yes."

She smiled at him and he smiled back. She wasn't

going to waste any more time doubting her decision. After all, she'd chosen life.

"ED? JAZZ?" MICHAEL banged on the door a couple more times, then stepped back as he heard the lock click.

"What are you banging for?"

"I need to speak to Ed."

"He's busy."

"I'm sure he is. But I need to speak to him."

Jazz looked behind him, then sighed. "Wait." He shut and locked the door.

Michael smiled at Tate as he waited, trying to make her see that this meeting was in her best interest, but she didn't look persuaded. All he could do was tell her the truth.

The lock clicked once more and the door opened just a bit.

"Turn around and give me your wrists."

Michael just wanted to talk to Ed, so he made no noises. It was logical that they'd given up on handcuffs with him, but damn, they could have used softer rope.

Jazz tied him up tighter than a turkey, then held his gun on him as he turned. "Don't do anything funny."

"I'm serious as a heart attack," Michael said.

Ed Martini was sitting in his favorite chair. Charlie looked even worse than he had before, and it made Michael wonder if it was strictly withdrawal that had him so torn up.

"What do you want?" Martini asked.

"She needs clothes."

Ed laughed. "I need more hair."

"If you're taking her to the bank, she needs to look

like she's there legitimately. She can't do that in the clothes she has."

Ed looked at Jazz, his smile fading, then back at Michael. "What kind of clothes?"

"She'll make a list. With sizes and designers."

"You knock again, hand the list to Jazz."

"When?"

"Tonight. And don't get any ideas about doing something while we're docked. I've already decided that whenever this boat stops, you're going to be inconvenienced. Or, if you don't stay where I put you, dead."

"Got it."

"Do the list."

Michael turned, then stopped. "I'm going to ask for a couple of things for myself."

"Yeah?"

"Yeah. I don't want to make her regret her feelings about me. So I need to look nice. Smell nice."

"Fine."

"We'd both appreciate some more to eat. And to drink."

Ed sighed. "Want a fucking massage while we're at it?"

Michael turned. "You need her. You need me. We're not asking for anything outrageous."

"Get the hell out of here," Ed said, his cheeks red, his eyebrows lowered.

Jazz shoved him in the back with the barrel of his gun, then made him stand at the doorway to the cabin while he undid the ropes. A second shove, and the door clicked shut.

Michael rubbed his wrists as he moved toward Tate,

who was standing at the porthole, staring out at the dark night.

"Can you see anything?"

"No, not really. But it beats staring at the wallpaper," she said, "or the vanity or the dresser or the bathroom."

He touched the small of her back. "I need you to make a list of clothes and whatever. Don't skimp and be very specific. If you want a certain brand, ask for it. Clothes you'd wear on holiday, knowing you'd be going to your bank."

She leaned back into his hand. "Makeup and hair, too?"

"I'm pretty sure we're going to dock in Miami or the Keys, so the shopping won't be an issue. Say what you need. He doesn't care if he spends twenty grand of the ransom if it means he gets the big prize."

She didn't say anything, but when she turned, she kissed him. Not too long, not too deep. A hint of things to come.

FORTY MINUTES AFTER Jazz came for her very complete and somewhat embarrassing list, there was another knock. Michael sent her to the far side of the room before he opened the door. It was Jazz again, with a tray. Michael took it; Jazz locked up behind him.

Michael put the tray on the bed, and when she registered what Jazz had brought, she looked at Michael with new respect. "Lobster tails and wine?"

"It helps to be the squeaky wheel," he said.

"A tip to file for future use."

"Want to talk or eat?"

She smiled as they crawled up on the bed together. It was odd to eat here, to sit next to Michael, to be a prisoner with such good wine. Everything felt off, but not in the way she'd expected.

Her fear remained, pulsing in her bloodstream, but somehow she still could function. Was this what Dr. Bay had wanted for her? Not the real kidnapping but this functional panic, this total awareness that she could die any moment, which made every nondeath moment something extraordinary?

"Hey," he said.

She realized she'd been looking his way—staring, really—but not seeing him. Quickly she averted her gaze. "Sorry."

"No need. I was just wondering what was going on in there."

"Random thoughts. I really like this wine."

"Those weren't food-review thoughts," he said, then shook his head. "It's fine if you don't want to tell me. None of my business."

"It's okay. I was thinking about my ability to talk. To eat, to smile, to sleep. I'd never have guessed."

"We're pretty adaptable creatures."

"Maybe it wasn't such a horrible idea to be kidnapped. Well, not by these louts but by someone safe."

His expression darkened. "No, it wasn't a good idea. None of this was. There was no way you should have been exposed to the possibility of danger."

"No? The only way to avoid it was to trade my life for safety. You think it was worth it?"

He looked at the dresser. "There had to be another way."

"Michael…" She put her glass down on the tray. "I wanted to ask you out—well, in—for five and a half months. I'm not talking about wanting to seduce you, I'm talking about dinner. A drink. I was frozen. My fear had leached into every single area of my life. From work to friends to dating. I was as much a prisoner in my apartment and that damn limo as I am here."

His gaze had come back to her face, to her eyes. She was glad there were no sunglasses. Just his vivid, open stare. Finally, after a long while, he blinked. Frowned. "You didn't want to seduce me?"

She laughed as she felt her face heat with a blush. He didn't shift his gaze, not even a bit, and every instinct told her to look away. But she was through being scared. At least of Michael.

# 13

HER FACE CAME ALIVE with her blush. It made her look young, innocent. She was, in fact, both of those things, but in her day-to-day life where she was the administrator of millions of dollars, where she was William Baxter's only daughter—where she was terrified from morning till night—she looked and acted much older, and her innocence hid behind a mask of tension.

She kept wanting to look away, but every time her gaze skittered, she forced herself to stay with him. The moments ticked on, marked by the sounds of their breaths, the motion of the boat. He waited as patiently as possible for Tate to relax, and finally she did.

It was eventually okay to do what he'd wanted to for a long time. He leaned in, slowly so she'd have time to adjust or, if she chose, to stop him. Her eyes stayed open until her breath, fruity with wine, brushed his mouth.

Only then did he close his own eyes as he touched his lips to hers. Again he had to wait, to let her adjust, which wasn't easy. His body urged him to take her, to toss the trays on the floor and do every kind of wicked thing to her. But his body wasn't in control. Not this time.

Tate needed a patient, gentle hand. Not something

he was accustomed to offering, but he'd do his best. He didn't want to spook her. That would be a crying shame for both of them.

It felt odd, this closed-mouth kiss, as if he was standing just outside the candy store. When he couldn't stand it another second, he parted his lips just a bit, then slipped his tongue out for a taste of her.

Mistake.

The rest of him really, really wanted to play. First thing, though—the trays.

As if diving into an icy stream, he pulled away quickly before he could change his mind. Her soft, disappointed moan made his dick, which was already paying attention, strain for more.

He put his tray to the side of the bed, then he practically sprinted out himself. Both trays ended up on the dresser, but then he was faced with another dilemma. Undress? Stay clothed? Undress her?

She was watching him, her blush back, and damn if she didn't lick her lips. Maybe if he took off his shirt. Her gaze shifted up, to the lights above them.

He shook his head at his own stupidity. Of course she'd want the lights out. It was Tate. The moment the room darkened he heard her sigh. A good sign. The sound of clothes shifting, a better one.

IT MADE ED NAUSEOUS to even look at Charlie. He gave Jazz a questioning glance, but Jazz, he was on the phone, making arrangements. Jazz was itching for a promotion, and Ed was running out of excuses to let him go. Jazz and him, they'd been together a long time. The boy was nuts, but he could control himself for Ed.

Jazz had recommended Ricky from his Brooklyn off-track parlor to take his place, but Ricky smelled like pickles all the damn time.

His gaze went back to Charlie. What a fucking loser. He had a shower that worked in his cabin, there were clothes that were clean in that room. So why was he still stinking up the saloon? His hair was stringy and he had gunk on the side of his mouth. It was enough to make a man lose his lunch.

If it wasn't for his usefulness in controlling the brother, he'd toss the bastard over right now.

"We'll be docked by three," Jazz said, folding his little phone and putting it in his pocket. "I've lined up a shopper to put together the stuff for the woman. Pauly's got the food being delivered at five. We'll be ready to take off by ten o'clock, latest."

"Good job. Did you tell Pauly I wanted those limes?"

"Absolutely, boss. He knows how much you like that key lime pie."

"Good. That's the pleasure of traveling without a woman—nobody to nag me about my damn cholesterol. She don't know what my cholesterol is. She just wants to control me, you know?"

"Yeah, I know. That's why I don't hook up for longer than a weekend. So is this Cayman Islands like Aruba?"

"I was only there once. But, yeah, it's like Aruba. Only with more banks. And more businesses. Lot of businesses."

Jazz raised his eyebrows. "They do off-track?"

"I don't know, Jazz. It's something to look into once we get the dough."

Jazz, always on his feet, so much energy, so much

going on in that bizzaro brain. The opposite of Charlie, who couldn't string two sentences together, who thought of nothing but himself, nothing but what he wanted that second. Like a five-year-old, that one. It made Ed wonder which of the brothers was adopted. Had to be one of them.

"Charlie," Jazz said, poking the listing slob on his shoulder. "Go to the cabin, would ya? You're making me lose my appetite."

"Fuck you, Jazz."

Jazz had his weapon out in two seconds. "What's that?"

"Nothing, nothing." He lurched toward the edge of the banquette and stumbled to his feet. "I thought you were someone else."

"Well, get the hell out of here before I throw you overboard."

Ed watched Charlie until he was out of the saloon.

"We have to keep him, boss?" Jazz asked. "I can make the brother behave. I can make the bitch behave. Trust me."

Ed shook his head. "No, I don't think you can. Those two, they've got some strength, okay? We need Charlie. Just until I'm off the boat with the woman. You can stay behind and watch the brothers kill each other."

"That," Jazz said, smiling, "I'd pay a nickel for."

HOW LONG HAD THE dark scared her? It felt as if it had been her whole life. The dark held secrets and bad things, terror and helplessness. Only, she didn't feel scared. Well, not that kind of scared. She was with

Michael and they were going to make love. Finally, at the edge of her life when she wasn't sure about the next sunrise or the next five minutes, she was sure about him.

Her hands found the bottom of her shirt and she pulled it over her head.

The room wasn't pitch-black. In fact, she could see him standing at the foot of the bed. Not his expression, not the small details, but enough. So she was pretty sure he could see her, too. He knew she was undressing and why.

As she moved to undo the clasp of her bra, Michael seemed to snap out of whatever had held him so still, directly into fourth gear. Before she'd gotten the bra off, he was down to his shorts. She couldn't make out the pattern in the dark, which was a blessing.

She tossed her bra to the floor, her blush coming back in spades. But this was her brave life, and she wasn't going to let her shyness stop her. In fact...

She climbed off the bed to stand in front of Michael. It was tempting to tell him to turn on the light—but, no, she wasn't that brave. Not yet. But she did continue to take off her clothes. Every last stitch.

And there they were.

He had the physique of a Greek athlete, which wasn't a shock, considering how serious he was about his workouts. She felt very soft and flabby in comparison. She should have worked harder at her Pilates, that's what.

"You're so beautiful," he whispered.

"Me?"

He laughed softly as he stepped closer. "Yes, you. You're incredibly beautiful. I like seeing you with your guard down. Without those suits you like so much."

"I like them because they blend in. They make me disappear."

"I know." He stepped closer, so close she could feel his body heat. "I like you like this. Naked. Vulnerable."

She did feel vulnerable. Too much so. She started to cover her breasts, but then he touched her. One hand on her waist, cool, broad, and the side of his other hand lifting her chin.

"And so very brave," he said.

She looked into his eyes, cursing the dark now. "I'm working on it."

"You're doing great," he said. Just before he kissed her.

She melted against him. His lips, his tongue, the pressure of his hand on the back of her head…it was all perfect. He made her wet and eager and braver still.

She put her hand on his stomach then, kissed him back as she went lower and lower until she felt the small patch of hair down there. A second later he bumped her wrist. She smiled around his tongue as it happened again. Someone wanted attention. Badly.

He moaned, and that's all the push she needed. She touched his cock. Warm, hard, thick and so very, very anxious. He pulsed in her hand. Strained as she stroked him.

He threw his head back for a second with a long groan, then pulled her to the bed. Before she knew what had happened, she was lying down, her head on the pillow, with Michael at her side, pulling her into his arms, into his kiss.

His leg went between hers, his thigh up to the

junction, where he pressed against her. She had no choice but to move, to ride him as he touched her breast, sucked her tongue. They went on like that for long, languorous moments. A gasp or a moan the only break in the accompaniment of their breathing. It was heaven, but it was also not quite enough.

She squeezed his cock, then let go, afraid she'd gone too far.

Michael sat up so quickly she gasped, and he gripped her shoulders tightly. When his mouth was a scant inch from her own, he said, "I can't stand it. I'm just not that strong."

His kiss was searing, melting her brain and stealing her breath. His body felt hard and hot.

Another man touching her with his fierceness would have made her cry out, struggle to break free, but she wanted Michael's possessiveness. A part of her wanted to see bruises, proof, in whatever tomorrow she was granted.

He moaned and she could taste his desire painted on her tongue. The sound of his rough breathing, all through his flaring nostrils, was like sex itself. Even the pulse of his chest against hers made her think of nothing so sweet as making love but of something far more primal. That's what she wanted from him.

William Baxter's troubled daughter. The one who was always pale and frail and didn't know what to do with her hands.

She knew now.

Trembling, still matching him breath for breath, she touched his skin, rubbed him, kneaded his flesh. There was so little give it disappointed her for a moment, but then she remembered it was Michael, not some soft man. He had muscles, big ones—not that you could see from across the room, but when you got close, when he moved—

He pushed her down to the bed, to the blue-and-white checked bedspread. His knee went between hers once more, but this time it was completely different. This time he didn't ask, he took.

Before her cry had subsided, he pulled her hands up above her head. With his broad left hand he captured both her wrists.

She stared at him as he loomed over her, a willing captive. "What are you doing to me?"

"I don't want you to forget this. If we die tomorrow, you'll remember this in your next life. In all your lifetimes."

He held her gaze as his mouth opened into a silent roar and he plunged inside her.

He filled her completely, but that wasn't why she wept. The tears were from somewhere very deep, something always longed for, and finally, finally…

He kissed her again, and it was brutal until it wasn't. Until he caressed her lips with his own, until there was no space between his breath and hers.

He was as deeply inside her as he could be. Michael was part of her. She would have shared her blood with him, her bones, but she didn't need to because he was right there. *Right there.*

MICHAEL, BURIED IN wet heat, didn't really understand what was happening to him. He'd wanted to make this special for her. He'd wanted to be careful, gentle.

Shit. He hoped he wasn't screwing it up, because there was no way he was gonna stop now.

He'd never been a patient man, not when it came to sex. Most of the time, he was on his way from one danger to another, so he'd mastered the art of the sentimental goodbye. Better to leave them wanting more, right?

But this…. Tate was another thing altogether. He'd been with more beautiful women. Certainly tougher women. She was vulnerable in a way that made him vulnerable, too.

He kissed her, wanting the thoughts to stop. She was so responsive. Just listening to her could have made him come. He had to hold back, to not hurt her, but his resolve lasted seconds. And when he did hurt her, she pushed him for more.

They would be gone by tomorrow, heading out across the ocean to the Caymans. His glorious plan hadn't turned out so well. Nothing had. Except this.

He'd never felt more of a failure—and he'd never experienced a triumph like being inside her.

He lifted his head, took in great, deep breaths, pumped into her until his arms shook. And then he reached between them, sliding his right hand down her belly until his fingers found her clit.

He watched her as he shifted his position, thrusting and rubbing her at the same time.

God, it was amazing. There was just enough light. Her eyes weren't closed, but they weren't focused, not on him anyway. Her mouth had opened as she'd arched her neck. It was stunning. He licked the sweat off her temple because he couldn't lick where he wanted.

Her head thrashed, banging against the wall as he kept up an unrelenting pace, but he knew it was going to end soon. He could feel the tightness in his balls, his muscles tensing beyond endurance.

He had to choose: finger or cock. Cock won.

He pulled his hand out, captured her wrists again, and when he felt her heels on his hips, he goddamn exploded. The top of his head came off, the backs of his eyelids burst with colors, and she just kept squeezing him, her internal muscles sucking the life force out of him.

It seemed to go on forever. When he was finally dry, when there was nothing, not even breath left in him, he opened his eyes.

She was staring up at him with those wide blue eyes. With her auburn hair plastered against her skin, her cheeks blotchy and red. He couldn't imagine anything more beautiful. Not even close.

Too soon, his arms gave out and he had to crash beside her. She didn't speak; neither did he, but the sound in the room was loud enough to scare the fishes. Both of them gasping for air, cursing the world that made them need it.

"Holy cow," she whispered finally.

He grinned. "Yeah, that's just what I was gonna say."

She slugged him in the hip. It was a lackadaisical sock with only half a fist. But good for her. He doubted he could have done better.

"Sleep now," he said.

"Uh-huh."

"Tomorrow we'll figure out how to live through this."

"Okay," she said, and even in her breathlessness, her doubt came through.

He rallied himself to his side, so his hand rested on her belly and his gaze on her eyes. "You think I want this to be over?" he said. "You think I'm not going to fight for you?"

She blinked. Then she smiled. "Not anymore."

# *14*

IT HAD BEEN DAYS—five days—since the kidnappers had disappeared with William Baxter's money and Tate. Sara, who'd never had a sister but had always had Tate, was sitting in her friend's bedroom, staring at the trompe l'oeil window on the wall. Through the painted window she could see a sandy beach, a brilliant ocean and a sky dotted with cotton clouds. It was so real that Sara thought if she moved closer, she would feel the breeze on her face.

But it, like the chances that Tate was still alive, was an illusion. There was a lot of trompe l'oeil throughout the penthouse, designed specifically to make the occupant feel as though she were living in an expansive world. The artist had done a superb job, but now Sara wondered if these fake paintings had been one more wall that had trapped Tate in her mental prison.

It wasn't fair. None of it was. That she should have been kidnapped at all, that she'd lived so much of her life in terror, that her cousin had been murdered in such a horrible way. Sara ached for Tate, but she also ached for William, who'd done so much to foster Tate's fear.

He'd aged ten years in these last few days. He couldn't sleep, wouldn't take the tranquilizers his doctor had prescribed and barely ate. Sara had taken a leave of absence from her job to be with him. To wait. But for how long?

Was Michael dead, too? Or was he, as William thought, one of the guilty?

Two days ago, she'd taken the bull by the horns. Despite her belief in Michael's team, she'd called the authorities. The FBI had swooped in, but they hadn't found much. She'd tried to believe them when they said they'd find Tate.

Sara stood up, knowing she had to go into the other room, face William as he waited another day by the phone. She had to keep things upbeat, if not for his sake then for her own.

She missed her best friend.


"Are you sure this is a good idea?" Charlie asked, trying not to sound too desperate. Jazz liked it when he could hurt people, and even though no one was gonna be beat up or anything, it was gonna be ugly.

"Just take the damn tray, would you? Jesus, you're such a whiny bitch."

"I haven't seen Mikey since—"

"I don't give a rat's ass. I'm busy."

Charlie sighed, but only after his back was to Jazz. He was so sick of this boat he wanted to scream. They'd already gotten the ransom money, so why in hell hadn't they just let him go? Why had Jazz given him that fix so he'd be out of it when they set out to sea?

He picked up the tray and headed to Mike's cabin. The cups rattled, but he couldn't help it. Mikey was gonna kill him, and Charlie already felt like crap. He knew there was some crack on board, but would they let him have any? Hell, no. They saw he wasn't doing so good, so it was just pure mean that made them act so shitty. And after he'd made them rich! The bastards.

"Well?"

Charlie jumped at Jazz's voice so close. He hadn't heard the dude walking, let alone opening the cabin door. "Shit."

"Do not piss me off, Charlie."

With as much indignation as he could muster, Charlie walked past Jazz into Mikey's cabin.

His brother stood up so fast he knocked an empty water glass off the bedside ledge. "What the hell?"

"Relax. I'm just bringing you something to eat."

"Get out of here, Charlie."

"I will. Just let me put this down." He went to the vanity, and as he was depositing the tray, the door to the cabin shut. It was Jazz screwing with him, making it easy for Mikey to wail on him. He turned, fast, but Mike was already in his face.

"How many people are on board?" Mike asked, his voice low, threatening.

"How should I know?"

Mikey's elbow bent and his arm went back. There was no mistaking the intent of his fist. "Count them."

"All right, all right. Me, Jazz, Martini, the cook, the pilot guy and some kid that cleans up."

"What are they planning?"

"You think I know? I shouldn't even be here. They was supposed to let me out when we brought the money. They tricked me!"

"Gee, I feel real bad for you there, Charlie."

"Look, I told ya—"

"I know exactly what you told me. And what you did. And what you're gonna do now."

Charlie shook his head, trying to inch toward the door. "I gotta go. They catch me talking to you, it's trouble all around."

"Don't you fucking move," Mikey said, pressing his body closer. "You tell me right this minute how many weapons are on board."

"I don't know."

"Charlie, I swear to God—"

"Mikey, I don't know. On Ma's grave, I don't know. They keep me in the dark."

"Then find out."

Charlie was sweatin' now. He could feel it dripping on his forehead, down his back. "I can't, Mikey. Don't ask me, 'cause I can't. You know I can't lie worth shit."

"You managed to lie to me."

"No, no I didn't."

"Find out, Charlie. Every single gun, rifle, harpoon, knife—you hear me? You find out and you get that information to me. If you try to pull something, I swear on Pa's grave, I will hunt you down and I will hurt you worse than you could ever believe."

"Yeah? Well, Martini will kill me. He's already threatened to throw me overboard."

His brother's arm went back, and Charlie flinched, but the punch never came. When he opened his eyes, he saw the woman behind Mikey, touching his shoulder. Shit, he hadn't even seen her when he walked in.

She looked different. Better. Pretty. No wonder Mikey liked his job so much. Must be sweet to get to work with a rich broad who looked like that.

"Get out, Charlie. Get out, and if you know what's good for you, you'll get me what I want to know."

"I'll try. That's all I can do."

Mikey spun around and Charlie wasted no time getting the hell out of there. Back in the saloon, Jazz was smiling like he'd been to the circus.

"Have a nice visit?"

Charlie almost told him what for, but he didn't. "No."

"What does he want you to do?"

He shouldn't say. Mikey was his brother, after all. His own blood. On the other hand, Martini had never liked him much. And Jazz? He was a goddamn psycho. "He wanted to know how many people were on board. How many guns."

"What did you tell him?"

"I didn't tell him nothing. I swear. I said I don't know, 'cause I don't."

Jazz gave him the once-over. "Watch your step, Charlie. It's a big ocean out there."

Charlie went out on the deck, staring at that ocean and planning how when Jazz wasn't looking, *he'd* be the one to go swimming. Next time he wouldn't tell Jazz a damn thing. He'd show them. Stupid rat bastards. Soon as he got home, he was gonna go to Len Taub's off-track parlor. Screw Ed. Screw Jazz.

TATE WASN'T SURE what to do. It wasn't easy watching Michael pace, so angry the vein on his forehead throbbed. But he also seemed to be working something out, at least from the bits and snatches of his mumbles that she caught.

Today was the first time she'd looked at Charlie. Jazz had brought them everything since that day she'd learned that Charlie and Michael were brothers. It had been upsetting, seeing them together, at least at first, but then, watching their interaction after spending so much time with Michael...she knew that she'd been right to believe him.

Michael might be good at his intelligence work, but he wasn't Olivier. He couldn't have made up his rage at Charlie. God, they were so different. Like night and day.

She decided she wasn't going to say a word. Let Michael pace, let him swear and plot and plan. While he was occupied, she took one of the sandwiches from the tray Charlie had brought, then she went to the bed and got the notebook she'd asked for two days ago.

It wasn't anything special, just an unlined notepad, but it was better than writing on the walls. Jazz had been reluctant to give it to her, too. Why, she had no idea. Who was going to see it? A passing sailfish?

Anyway, she curled her legs underneath her, got the pillow behind her back and turned to a new blank page.

"Dear Sara," she wrote, remembering where she'd left off. "Jazz brought a bunch of shopping bags into the room, then left us to sort through them. I was thrilled to find underwear—although, jeez, the slime-ball had gotten the most revealing things he could find. I swear, it looked more like he'd shopped at Frederick's of Hollywood than Victoria's Secret. Michael didn't seem to mind, but he played it cool.

"There's simply no way to forget why we're here. It's not a pleasure cruise, and there's no beach party waiting for us in Grand Cayman.

"I'm just grateful Michael is with me. He thinks he's failed, that he's responsible for what's happened. I can't agree. It wasn't his fault he had Charlie for a brother. But I can't seem to make Michael stop worrying about it and save his strength for when we dock.

"Personally, Sara, I think the real truth is that this whole thing was my fault. And before you say it, yes, I think Dr. Bay was more than idiotic. What I mean… You know the old saying 'You reap what you sow'? Well, I've been 'sowing' being kidnapped since Lisa. I know it makes sense that I was obsessed, but I didn't do near enough to get myself out of that insidious loop.

"I was given tremendous gifts and I squandered them to live in the land of what-if. No more. I am here, today. I am with Michael and he is with me. Together, we're strong. Even me.

"I—"

He sat in front of her, making her pen jolt like a lightning bolt up the page. "I should have killed him when I had the chance."

She hid her gasp as he said the words, his face showing her that it wasn't an idle threat. "Don't."

"Don't what? He got you kidnapped, Tate. He stole from me and he's probably going to get me killed. If I don't do something about it, we'll both die, and it'll be because of Charlie."

"It doesn't matter."

"What?"

"It doesn't matter that he did all this. You can't kill him. He's your brother."

"Not anymore."

"He'll always be your brother."

Michael stood up again. "No. I've done everything I could to help him. I've bailed him out of jail, I've given him money for his bookies, I've spent thousands putting him in rehab. He just wants more and more, and I have no more to give."

"Still—"

"Tate, if it was just me, I could see cutting him a little slack, although it wouldn't be for him but for my father. But to put you here? No. It's over. It stops. Now."

"I understand. I really do. But you'll have to live with whatever choice you make."

He smiled at her with a tenderness that made her melt. "I will do whatever it takes to keep you safe. Period. Now are you going to keep writing in that journal or are you going to take my mind off the rest of the universe?"

"Oh, you want to play charades?"

"Ha. You're funny." He slipped the notebook from her fingers and tossed it to the floor. The pen was dispatched next.

Then it got really interesting.

SHE SLEPT AS HE TORE a couple of pages from her notebook and found the pen where he'd tossed it hours before. The longer they remained on the boat, the more he worried that he'd never get her home.

The whole reason he'd come up with the idea of the Cayman bank was to give himself time. But had that backfired? Were there so many armed men on the boat that he couldn't take them?

The fact that he even thought that bothered him more than he could admit. Last year, would he have hesitated? Would he have given this motley crew a second thought?

He could take Martini and Jazz. As long as he knew where they were and no one jumped him from behind, there was no contest. But there were other people on board, and he had no idea where they would be at any given time.

He hadn't been a complete slouch. At night, when Tate was asleep, he'd done something in the way of recon. He'd only been out of their cabin twice, but he'd gotten a lot of information on both silent trips.

The first, he'd gotten a damn good idea about the saloon and the outer perimeter of the boat. He drew what he remembered now in a diagram that would help him put together the pieces he hadn't seen.

Charlie and Jazz had been asleep that night, the night before last. Charlie, snoring. Neither had stirred as he'd walked past them, and it had been harder than hell not to take the gun from Jazz's splayed hand and shoot him beyond recognition.

He'd held himself back. He might have been outside the cabin, but the boat was still mostly unknown. With Tate so vulnerable, he had to make sure. If he'd been killed, her chances for survival were slim. So he'd inched around quiet as a mouse as he'd used the full moon to check for possibilities.

Last night hadn't gone quite as well.

He'd made it halfway to the cockpit when Ed had come up from below. For what felt like an hour Michael had stowed himself in a ridiculously narrow gulley behind a couch. He'd learned nothing except that Ed Martini liked to cuss at televised sports.

When he finally got a chance to get back to the room, his leg had cramped and he'd missed being caught by a quarter of a second.

Tate had slept through it all, which was what he'd wanted.

He couldn't be sure when they'd reach Grand Cayman, but both of them had to be ready, starting tomorrow. He had to have plans made, with contingencies. The one he hated the most was where they would take Tate away, off the boat, alone.

She thought she was ready. That she could handle it. He knew better.

He finished the rudimentary diagram of the boat, but he knew if there was a cache of weapons on board, they would be below and they'd be under lock and key. But if he had a gun, any kind of gun, their chances of surviving this would be a lot better.

He turned to the bed. She looked beautiful with her hair in a halo on the pillow. Odd, a woman of such privilege and she never complained about the living conditions. He knew, far too well, all the things that made her life so different from regular folks'. She had a cadre of beauticians, aestheticians, nail people, wax people, makeup people who came to the penthouse on a steady schedule. He didn't know what half of them did except make her look great.

Aside from her looks, she had maids, cooks, him. She never had to get her hands dirty. Someone was always there to clean up her messes.

She looked better here, though. He'd never even known her hair was wavy. Or that she really liked peanut-butter-and-jelly sandwiches.

As he watched her sleep, he let himself think about after. Once they were back in New York, on her turf. Would she be embarrassed by the fact that she'd slept with her bodyguard? Would she pretend nothing had ever happened? Would he?

It wasn't as if they would ever be anything. Not a couple, that's for sure. William would have heart failure if such a thing were even suggested. Too bad. He'd liked her from the start, and being with her in this cramped cabin for all this time had just proved he'd been right in his earliest assessments.

Tate was an unusual woman, and not just because of her social standing. One thing he'd seen in his travels was that the children of the truly rich didn't understand the rest of the world. They made noises about helping out the disenfranchised or the handicapped, whatever, but it was all posing. They lived in rarefied air, and those who weren't like them were as foreign as Martians.

Tate was the exception to the rule. She'd never made him feel as if he were the help. Not intentionally, anyway. Hell, she hadn't even wanted to admit how badly he'd bungled things with her, even though his mistakes might cost her her life.

So what was a man supposed to do with a woman like that? Save her, that's what. Make damn sure she had the opportunity to find out what life would be like without her fear of being kidnapped overshadowing everything.

He had to find those weapons. Now.

# 15

THE FBI AGENT'S NAME was Webber, Nick Webber, and he called Sara at four in the afternoon on the ninth day. "We might have something."

"Go on."

"We think it might be her purse. There's no ID, but there's a GPS tracker sewn into the lining. The security people said that's where Caulfield hid his trackers."

"I'll know if it's hers," Sara said. "But let's meet somewhere. I don't want Mr. Baxter to know."

"Fine."

"Where did you find it?"

"In Jersey, by the GW Bridge."

"That could mean anything. They could have her anywhere."

"It'll help to know if this is her bag."

"Give me twenty minutes and meet me at Sarabeth's. You know where that is?"

"Yes."

"Twenty minutes." Sara hung up the phone, her heart so heavy she could barely breathe. Was this all they were to have of Tate? A purse washed up from the East River? Was Tate in that murky water right now with the punctured tires and the polluted fish?

William was withering away before her eyes. He wouldn't eat, and the only sleep he got was drug induced. She'd taken her fair share of tranquilizers, too.

How long was she supposed to hang on? She wanted to believe so badly. So when was the cutoff? Ten days? Twenty? Or were they always supposed to feel that jolt when the phone rang? A year, two years, what did it matter? A purse was not proof. It was simply a purse.

THE DOOR HAD BEEN unlocked for a good thirty seconds, but Michael didn't turn the knob. He pressed his ear against the door, trying to decide whether the noise he heard was just the television—which was on all the time, as far as he could tell—or actual conversation.

At one-twenty in the morning, he couldn't imagine who'd be chatting. Those first few days they'd made a point to keep themselves awake, guns at the ready, especially after his first attempt at escape. But the last couple of nights Jazz and Charlie had both been sound asleep and not even the louder-than-loud commercials from the satellite system had made them budge.

He couldn't tell whether tonight would be an exception, so he opened the door. Not wide—Jesus, no—but just enough so he could let his eye adjust to the light as he peered through the gap.

He didn't see Jazz, but there was Charlie, leaning back in the big man's favorite leather chair, mouth agape, snoring like a freight train. Even now, after everything, Michael's first instinct was to get Charlie out of that chair. If Ed saw him there...

It was just so goddamn typical. Charlie would never

change. If Michael could figure out a way to get him out of this mess, it wouldn't matter because there would be the next mess and the one after that. It made him sad—but not sad enough to forgive. That wasn't going to happen.

Another few seconds of absolute stillness, then he opened the door another inch. Still no Jazz. Surely they wouldn't leave Charlie on guard duty by himself? No one was that stupid.

Someone else had to be there. Or in the head or maybe getting something to eat in the galley. Whatever, it meant that tonight Michael wasn't going to make it below. He wasn't going to get a weapon, at least not yet.

He closed the door, locking it behind him, then debated the wisdom of getting into bed. Tate was hard to resist, but he wanted to check back in an hour to see if he could make it out. An hour of either sleep or something better wouldn't be prudent. He'd get too sleepy. Too satisfied.

"Are you just going to stand there all night?"

Tate's whisper scared the crap out of him, making him glad for the darkness. "What are you doing up?"

"Watching you be superspy. Like last night. And the night before."

He grinned as he headed to the bunk. "It's not nice to fool superspies."

"Hey, you're not the only one who can do that stealthy stuff. What's the matter? Someone's up?"

"I only saw Charlie. But they'd never leave him on his own. I'll check again in a while."

"Hmm," she said, scooting over as he sat on the edge of the bed. "How long is a while?"

He touched her cheek with the back of his hand. "It would be wonderful to climb in with you, but I don't think it's a good idea. We're getting too close to Grand Cayman, and either I get a decent layout of this boat or—"

"Or what?"

"Nothing. I'll get it. But I need to stay alert."

"I can do that, too."

"You should get some sleep."

"Because I lead such an active life? The only thing we do here that burns up calories is sex, and if you don't want to do that—"

"Who said I don't want to?"

She sighed. "I know. So what happens once we get there?"

"Ed's going to take you off the boat. You'll have to go with him to the bank."

"What about you?"

"I'll be taking care of business here. You don't have to worry about that."

She sat up, then leaned across him to turn on the light. She had on a T-shirt, which she wore most nights, and he wondered whether if they hadn't been afraid of Jazz barging in, she would have slept naked.

The thought of her long body next to his… Hell, they'd never get any rest.

Squinting against the light, she still managed to give him her "you're-in-trouble-now-mister" look. "I'll ask again. What about you?"

"There are things I can do once we're docked, once they can't use you as a shield."

"Like killing people."

"If necessary."

"Including Charlie."

"If necessary."

"They have weapons."

"I do, too."

"Where?"

He shrugged, wanting to reassure her as well as instill her with confidence. He wasn't sure he could do both. "I've been in a lot of situations where it looked as if I didn't stand a chance."

"But—"

He put his arm around her shoulder and situated them both more comfortably on the bed. "Let's talk about you for a while, okay? There are some things I want you to practice here, while we're alone, before you hit the bank."

"Like breathing? Not passing out?"

He shook his head. "You're going to be fine. You've been amazing, and there's no reason that shouldn't continue."

"Except that I won't be with you."

"Doesn't matter."

She looked into his eyes. "Are you kidding? Of course it matters. You're the only reason I'm not completely comatose. Or dead."

"You may have gotten some confidence with me nearby, but you've done so much on your own. You don't even break a sweat when they bring in the food."

"I do so."

"It doesn't show."

She sighed. "Not that much has changed, Michael. We're living in a bubble here where it's easy to pretend. But once I have to leave this room… If you're counting on me, you'd better rethink things."

"Don't worry about it. The plan is only viable if you think it'll work. There are too many unknowns to get too specific."

"Well, let's hear what it is. If I don't pass out now, then maybe I won't pass out in the bank."

AT TWO-FORTY, MICHAEL came back to the room. There was enough light from the porthole for her to see the foray hadn't been terrific.

"What happened?"

He came to the edge of the bed, stripping as he walked. His T-shirt hit the floor along with the jeans they'd bought him in Florida, leaving him in his skivvies. "Charlie lied again."

"Oh, no."

"Oh, yes. I thought I was home-free, everyone accounted for, and was just about to pick the lock where I'm sure the weapons are stored when that cabin boy he talked about—the one who was supposed to clean up—came walking out of the head. He's monster-size. Thank God he flushed or I'd have been very damaged."

"I'm very grateful you're not damaged." She threw the covers back and patted the bed. "But now you need to get some sleep."

"Let me get washed up. Don't move."

By the time he'd finished brushing his teeth she'd worked herself into a small frenzy of worry. "You can't do this anymore," she said as he crawled in next to her. "It's too dangerous."

"I have to get to the weapons, Tate."

"Find another way. I won't be able to stand it if something happens to you."

He pulled her close, putting his arm under her neck, positioning himself so he could look into her eyes. "I'll be here," he said. "I won't leave you."

She believed him as best she could. The closer they came to the island, the worse her fears were becoming. Michael tethered her to the earth, to sanity. If he were gone—

"Hush," he said. "Stay with me. Don't be anywhere else but right here."

She nodded.

He kissed her. It was long and languid and she touched his skin wherever her hand landed. In the days and nights that had sailed by, she'd learned the heaven of familiarity, the comfort of knowing she couldn't make a mistake.

She pleased him. She knew it, and it brought her an extraordinary confidence. If she could bring that feeling to her whole world...

"A little help?"

She looked at him, startled out of her reverie. "With what?"

"Panties."

"I don't think they would look that good on you, but, sure, give it a try."

"Oh, you're hilarious."

"Come on, Michael," she said, turning her head fetchingly to the side. "Haven't you ever wanted to try a walk on the wild side?"

"The masculine wild side, sure. Panties? That's a big no."

"What a chicken. You'd probably look adorable."

"The last thing in the world I want to look like is adorable."

"Right. You're a lumberjack and you're—"

"Hold it right there. You want to see some wild-side action? How does a little spanking sound?"

"Hmm. Your bottom all red and rosy?"

"Not mine."

"Oh, then no. It sounds terrible."

His mouth opened, but no sound emerged. Finally he just shook his head.

"Don't worry, Michael. You don't have to understand. Just smile and say, 'Yes, dear.'"

"Yes, dear," he said as he dutifully smiled. "But just for the record, this isn't over."

"No?"

"It's just going to take me a while to figure out my strategy. I'm thinking a surprise visit in the middle of the night. Something kinky but not too startling."

"All for me?"

He nodded.

She pulled his head down so her mouth was an inch from his ear. "Add some leather to that mix, big guy, and I'm all in."

"Oh, shit," he said as he got to his knees and pulled her into a kiss that went on and on.

He didn't have to remind her again about the whole panty situation. She got naked, fast, tossing her clothes somewhere away, and then she got him naked, too.

By that time he was hard for her, hard all over. She liked to run her hands over his chest and feel the hard buds of his nipples beneath her palms. He liked it when she tweaked him there, and she was happy to oblige.

He'd figured out a lot of her favorite things, too. Like now, when he used two fingers to get her ready for the main event. And how he nipped at the tender skin just below her ear until she shivered with pleasure.

Then oddly, his pace slowed until she pulled back to look at him. "What's wrong?"

He shook his head, but the look he gave her was as pensive as she'd ever seen him.

"Michael?"

"I would never hurt you."

"I know that."

"Maybe. But I want to say it anyway. I miss a lot about my old life—the pace, the adrenaline. It was good for me and I was good at it. But meeting you…"

She swallowed and held her breath, afraid to speak or even breathe lest he stop.

"Meeting you has changed every damn thing. But I want you to understand something."

He held her tighter, bruising her arm. She didn't care, not at all.

"I'm going to get you out of this. And when you go back to your real life, you won't be the same person. You'll be stronger. Better."

His eyes searched hers with amazing intensity, but he was starting to scare her now. This wasn't the speech she'd hoped for. She didn't know how she knew, but she knew.

"I'm going to miss you. But I want you to know I'll be rooting for you to have the life you deserve. You will. You'll be able to travel. It kills me to say it, but you'll have your pick of men. The world will be yours. All you have to do is take it."

"So you think I can have any man I want?"

"I know it. You're beautiful, and that's the least of it. Don't you settle for anything less than the best, you hear me? Any man—the goddamn princes of the world—would be lucky to know you, let alone love you."

She couldn't have stopped her tears if her life depended on it. His sincerity slipped into her heart, and she knew it would be there forever.

He was also telling the truth. Not about the men who'd line up for her but that he wouldn't be in that line. This was going to end. One way or the other, Michael was going to leave her. She didn't want it to be so, but even a woman who'd lived most of her life in the land of magical thinking could see that he couldn't continue as her bodyguard. Not after all this.

"Tate?"

She sniffed. "Hmm?"

"We still have right now."

There was something so sweet about his voice, about his face. "Thank you," she said. "Thank you for being my safe place. For seeing so much in me. I'll never forget you."

"You'd better not," he said as he laid her down, as he moved between her legs. As he entered her body as completely as he'd entered her heart.

# *16*

THEY DOCKED AT FIVE that morning. Tate held on to Michael as she listened for new voices, a chance perhaps to get someone's attention.

He squeezed her shoulder and kissed her on the temple. She instantly calmed. Not Zen calm or anything, but she could feel the tension ease from her shoulders.

"I know it's wishful thinking on my part," she whispered after hearing nothing but Jazz's voice on deck, "but, hey, we have to try."

"We do, but I'd feel a lot better if you were off the boat. There's a much greater chance you can get away."

"I don't want to go."

"I know," he said.

"They're so damn secretive at the bank. We'll be taken into a private room. It's not like going to a bank in New York."

"Just do what we talked about."

"I'll try."

"You'll be great. I have complete faith in you."

"Well, that's just insane."

He laughed, then he tilted her chin up. There wasn't much light, not enough to make out every detail, and yet she could picture every inch of his face. She closed her eyes, holding the image still and strong so that when she was out there she could bring it back.

His kiss was gentle and sweet, a tender counterpoint to last night's urgency.

After the anchor went down, the boat rocked with a whole new motion. For two hours they lay entwined. Kissing sometimes, touching everywhere. She tried so hard not to think of this as the end, but she wasn't strong enough.

"Michael?"

"Yeah?"

"I know what you said last night makes sense, but I can't let it go. If… When we get back to New York, I want—" She felt him tense, and that made her stumble, but she really needed to say this now. "I want you."

His chest rose, but it didn't fall for too many heartbeats.

"Was that the wrong thing to say?"

He exhaled and pulled her closer. "No, not at all. I'm really flattered."

"Screw flattered. Talk to me."

"I'm going to resign," he said. "That's a given. But I doubt all will be forgiven. You're father's not going to be happy with me. And he's right. I was supposed to protect you and I put you in danger."

"You didn't."

"I did. Charlie is my fault. I should have cut him off years ago. I should have figured that he'd know how to break into my safe. I was stupid and you're paying for it."

"Okay, you have to stop that right now. I know you had nothing to do with Charlie's plan. You've put your own life at risk to take care of me. So don't even try to go there."

"Even if I don't, you're father already has."

"I'm not my father."

"And for that I'm most grateful."

"Michael. I'm not kidding around."

"I know you're not. And believe me, I'm goddamned amazed that a woman like you could want me. I just don't think you should make any promises. Not yet."

"I've run from promises my whole life. If I want to make one now, I will."

"Okay, then. Promise away."

"Please don't make light of this. I've never felt this way before. Not ever. You've been a revelation. Not just because you know how to make me tremble, but because—"

He didn't say anything. But he held his breath again.

"Because of how you see me. I had no idea this was even possible. All I can call it is simpatico. It sounds too fancy for what I mean, but—"

"No. I get it. I understand completely."

She allowed herself a little grin. "Told ya."

"Tell you what," he said. "When we get back, we'll take a look at how things stand. Just you and me. Okay?"

"Okay."

"Now try and sleep."

"Ha."

He kissed her temple one more time. "Rest, then. Rest."

FOR THE FIRST TIME since they'd kidnapped her, Ed came into the cabin. It was just past eight and she hadn't slept a wink. She'd been too busy thinking, not about the day ahead or what she'd have to face but about a future filled with Michael.

Of course, her father wouldn't approve, but that was too damn bad. She hadn't told him, not in so many words, but she loved Michael. Loved him in a way she'd never dreamed for herself.

"Get dressed," Ed said. "I want you ready in one hour."

He looked like an island millionaire. He wore an elegant Hawaiian shirt—which seemed contradictory but wasn't—khaki pants, deck shoes and a Panama hat to cover his bald spot. His tan was deep, his Rolex top-of-the-line, and the diamond on his pinkie could have been used as an anchor.

He turned to Michael. "Make sure she looks good."

Before Michael could say a word, Ed left, locking the door behind him.

She sat on the bed in her T-shirt. It was already starting. Her pulse pounded, her breathing grew labored. She closed her eyes so she wouldn't see the narrowing of her vision.

"Come on, kiddo," Michael said. "Don't project. One foot in front of the other. You need to shower, right? That's not scary. You've done that a thousand times before."

She nodded, then looked up at him as her thoughts took a right turn. "Michael, you have to promise me that you won't kill Charlie."

"What?"

"Promise me. I know you're going to fight and do all your spy stuff, and you can feed every one of these bastards to the sharks as far as I'm concerned, but you can't kill Charlie."

He straightened his back and flexed his jaw, and it was so easy to see the warrior in him. He'd been on his best behavior when her life had been at risk, but the moment she was off the boat... She tried to feel sorry for Jazz, but she couldn't. He deserved everything Michael would give him.

"Michael, please. If you do, you'll regret it forever."

"Don't ask me to make that promise, Tate."

"Why not?"

"I have no idea what I'm going to be facing once you're gone. Please don't tie my hands that way."

"All right. But will you try?"

"I will."

She stood and went right into his arms. "That's all I need."

He took her by the shoulders and looked at her with his green-gold eyes. "I need so much more."

There was nothing gentle about this kiss. She felt it to her toes, to her chromosomes. She needed to be strong for this. To come back to him.

He broke away. "Go on. Get ready. Remember, one step at a time."

It wasn't easy, but she managed to do just that. Shower, makeup, hair, the clothes Jazz had bought her in Florida. When she finally looked in the mirror, she knew she looked just as privileged as Ed. In fact, she looked as if she could have been his daughter.

It had been so easy to step back into the habits of

years. The hair not just curled but coiffed, after lessons
from some of the most sought-after stylists in the world.
The makeup might not have been hers, but she knew
how to work it. Subtle in every way. Elegant and under-
stated. To be flashy was to be vulgar. To be one of *them*.

And how would it be to live with—hell, date—one
of them? A man who was her chauffeur, for heaven's
sake? The talk would be incessant, the censure obvious
at every gathering. She didn't give one solitary damn,
as she'd never fit in anyway. But what about her
father?

He cared so very much. His life was a monument
to wealth and everything wealth brought. Including
this.

While Michael insisted on blaming himself, she
looked elsewhere. As much as she loved her father, her
kidnapping now seemed inevitable. After Lisa, it had
only been a matter of time.

He'd instilled in her a number of wonderful things:
her social responsibility, her respect for hard work. But
he'd also raised her to be a victim.

That she had spent so much of her time in captivity
not feeling like a victim was a tribute to Michael. And
herself. She couldn't forget that. She'd done re-
markably well, considering.

There was a brief knock at the bathroom door.
"Tate?"

This was it. She had to go out now, leave Michael
behind, act her ass off. She had to be strong and there
was no one to depend on but herself.

She took a deep breath and opened the door.

Ed was there along with Jazz. They looked her over

as if she were a prize pony. She felt the heat rush to her face, but she kept it together. Head up, shoulders back, an air of detachment. At least that part was easy.

"You look good. Now all you have to do is keep your mouth shut and sign the papers." Ed touched her hair and she didn't even flinch. "Make it look real, sweetheart, and you'll live to see another day."

Ed turned to Jazz and gave him a nod. Ed stepped closer to her and pulled a gun from the back of his waistband, while Jazz went to Michael's side, next to the bed.

"What's just as important," Ed continued, positioning the barrel of the gun in her side, "is that your boyfriend here might live, too."

Before she could even take a step or be scared about the gun, Jazz pulled Michael's right arm straight out, laid it palm up on the edge of the bedside counter and smashed it with the butt of his weapon. She heard the bone snap like a twig, followed instantly by Michael's sharp cry.

The blood drained from her head and she gasped for breath as she struggled not to throw up. She could see exactly where it was broken at the wrist.

She turned on Ed and slapped him across the face, the sound not nearly loud enough.

He lifted his weapon, his whole face red and furious. She knew he might pull the trigger, but all she wanted was to punish him for what he'd done, then turn her wrath on Jazz.

"Tate, no!" Michael, holding his arm tight against his side, stepped forward, his left arm out to pull her away.

Ed trembled as he stared at her and she could see

the war in his eyes. He wanted so badly to kill her, but it would cost him dearly. "You shouldn't have done that."

"You have no reason to hurt him. I've agreed to give you my money. That's what you're after. Not him."

Ed took another step closer, and now the barrel of the gun touched her temple, the same place Michael had kissed so tenderly. "If you try anything stupid again, I'm going to give Jazz here a call. He's going to break the other hand and then he's going to shoot out the right kneecap, then the left. By the time Jazz is finished there won't be a bone in his body that isn't broke. You got that?"

The thought brought up the bile in her throat, but she couldn't break down. Not now. "Yes."

"Good." He put the weapon back in his waistband, then covered it with his brightly colored Hawaiian shirt. "Let's go."

She looked at Michael's hand, already swelling. "He needs a doctor."

"When it's over," Ed said. "He'll get all the attention he needs. Come on."

He led her to the door, but just before she stepped through, Michael said, "Wait."

She turned.

"I love you," he said. "I think I have for a long time. Just know that, okay? Know it."

WALKING OUT OF THE room was like death. The sun shone warm on her skin, the water sparkled blue and the wind smelled of the sea—and it was all gallows.

She kept hearing that sickening snap over and over

in her head. All she wanted to do was kill Ed Martini and Jazz and, yes, Charlie, too, and get back to Michael. It hurt her that he was in pain, that Jazz could injure him so easily.

Too easily.

God, Michael had let that horrible man hurt him to protect her. Because Ed had the gun on her.

Her steps slowed, but Ed's hand on her back led her onto the small sea taxi, where he sat her down so close to him his aftershave filled her nostrils. She stared at the shore, at Seven Mile Beach, while Ed told her he was now her uncle Ed—Ed Martini, her father's best friend. That the money was being transferred to his account temporarily and that William would come soon to make different arrangements.

Then he made her repeat everything he'd said. By the time she'd done so for the fifth time, they had docked. As she stood, he touched her arm, her back, then her arm again, and it was all she could do not to slap him over and over until he took her back to the boat, to Michael.

She'd never felt this before, this rage so bright and hot that she knew without a doubt she could take his gun and blow him away. She'd never even guessed she had this murderousness in her. Her vivid imagination hadn't been enough. She'd always pictured herself as the victim, not the killer.

Although she hadn't been to Cayman in years, she remembered the soft white beaches here and how she'd enjoyed playing with the turtles and snorkeling. This memory would forever be overshadowed, however long forever turned out to be.

They walked, the two of them, past the seaside cafés

and shops, toward the center of town. Toward her bank. He held on to her each step of the way, hurting her as she passed one khaki-dressed police officer after another.

She said nothing. She obeyed and would obey. There was only one chance in a million she could get herself out of this, but she wasn't going to try even that. Not with Michael's well-being at stake.

He slowed her down as they crossed the street in front of Grand Cayman Bank. "Who am I?" he asked.

"Uncle Ed."

"Say it again—and smile this time."

She forced her lips to curve up. "Uncle Ed."

He walked into the shade on the right side of the street and took out his cell phone. With one push of his button he was on the phone with Jazz, and she was trembling. "Jazz, let's see what you can do to his left hand."

"No!" she said, but he yanked her back, close to a pastry shop window.

"Say it again."

She looked at him through a red haze of hatred, but she made herself smile, pretend this wasn't death, that Michael wasn't being hurt this very second. "Uncle Ed."

"Again."

"Uncle Ed."

"Better. Just don't forget I have the phone right here." He patted his pocket. "There's only one way he doesn't die, and die ugly."

IT HAD TAKEN MICHAEL too long to wrap his hand in the bathroom towel, to swallow half the bottle of aspirin. He knew Jazz would be coming back any minute, and when he did, there were going to be some changes.

Now that Tate wasn't directly in harm's way, he could do what he'd wanted to when Jazz had grabbed his wrist.

He went back to the bedroom. He could still unlock the door, even with his dominant hand out of commission. But that wasn't the plan. He needed Jazz to come in here.

Once he'd taken that prick out, he'd move on, but slowly. Each member of the crew had to be taken out before he'd blow the whistle on Martini.

On the one hand, he wanted Jazz to hurry the hell up. On the other, a few more minutes for the aspirin to take affect wouldn't hurt.

He cursed his luck for the hundredth time. Why had he bailed out Charlie so many times? Why'd he have to promise his father he'd watch out for that loser? And why the hell had he fallen in love with Tate Baxter?

There was no good outcome to this scenario. She didn't deserve any more anguish, not on his account. Goddamn, he was a fool.

He turned too sharply and pain radiated up his arm. Yeah, some more time for that aspirin would be just great. Was that Jazz? Shit, he had to be ready to do what needed to be done.

TATE SAT AT THE BANK vice president's desk, waiting for him to draw up the transfer papers. After 9/11, things had changed, even here, and there was a lot more red tape to tamp down on money laundering. If only they knew who Ed Martini really was. But they wouldn't discover the truth from her.

She'd smiled, answered questions, been attentive, but now she had to remember what Michael had told her. Even though it might be the wrong choice, she had to try. If she could stop Ed now, she could still get to Michael before Jazz had done too much damage.

She began with the breathing. Taking in larger and larger breaths.

"What are you doing?"

"I—"

He pinched her on the back of her arm, and she bit her lip so she wouldn't yelp.

"Stop it."

"I don't think I can."

He smiled broadly and leaned toward her, bringing his lips close to her ear. "First his right kneecap, then his left."

She breathed harder, deeper, faster, knowing she would hyperventilate and that would make her pass out. It was her only job, her only shot. To do what she'd done for years—have a panic attack, only this one had to be deliberate and it couldn't last hours. She had to faint, to be cared for by someone, anyone, except Uncle Ed.

He pinched her again. "Don't you fuckin' dare."

"Please, I can't help it. It's the agoraphobia. I have no...no control."

"You'd better find some, bitch. Or he won't have one—"

Mr. Granger, the vice president, reentered the room and Ed's face changed again. He looked up at the man with concern.

"Could you bring my niece a cup of water? She's not feeling well."

"Of course. One moment." He picked up his phone

and asked his secretary to bring fresh water. Before he hung up, he asked, "Is there anything else I can do?"

Ed shook his head. "No. She'll be fine."

Tate looked at him. Tried to smile. Then everything went black.

# _17_

MICHAEL STOOD JUST to the left of the door, waiting. His right hand, immobilized in a towel, was strapped to his back with the aid of two torn pillowcases. It felt weird, but he couldn't strap the hand in front—it would present too easy a target.

He didn't think he'd be fighting long. Jazz would come in, Michael would knock the crap out of him using his three remaining limbs and get the gun. The gun would make the rest of his job simpler still.

His only worry at this point was Tate. She was out there by herself. Michael hoped that Ed had ditched his weapon before going to the bank. He doubted very much even an offshore bank would appreciate a customer coming in with a loaded Glock.

But even if he didn't have a gun to use on Tate, he'd have no trouble getting her to sign the papers. Breaking his hand was the smartest thing Ed could have done. Tate wasn't used to these kinds of tactics and she had no idea what Michael was capable of.

How could she? He'd been so afraid of getting her hurt that he'd behaved like a civilian this whole trip. He'd been knocked out—twice—caught behind a sofa, tripped up by his brother. She probably thought he'd made up his military training.

He should have kicked ass and worried later. Even with Charlie here, with Tate so vulnerable. He'd never behaved this stupidly before, not on any mission he'd ever had. He'd have been drummed out of the Army for this.

There was a noise outside, a thump, and it brought him right back into the room, into this mission right here. He breathed deeply and evenly, balanced himself to make optimum use of what he had to work with. Jazz was going down. And if it was painful on the way, so much the better.

The lock turned and the door swung open. Michael waited until Jazz walked in, ready for anything. Only, it wasn't Jazz. It was Charlie. He was crying like a baby, but his gun, silencer and all, was pointed straight at Michael's chest.

TATE OPENED HER EYES. She didn't know where she was, who the man standing in front of her was, what was going on, and fear shot through her. She scrambled back, barely realizing she'd been lying on a leather couch, and then she saw Ed.

He made everything worse. Her chest seized, her vision narrowed. And she was pretty sure he wasn't going to get his money because she'd be dead any second.

"I'll call the hospital," the man said, his accent broad and his face terribly worried.

"No, it's all right," Ed said. "Just give us a moment. She's disoriented, that's all. She had a rough night on the boat."

The man eyed Ed, then her. "It won't take them but a moment—"

"No, thank you. We just need a few minutes alone."

"Very well. I'll be right outside if you need me."

"I appreciate it," Ed said, his smile looking so genuine it made Tate's pulse pound harder.

The moment they were alone, Ed's demeanor switched to his true self. Malevolent, angry, brutal. He got right into her face, his arms on either side of her. If he'd been a lover, he'd have swooped in for a kiss, but there was nothing but hate in his eyes, in the way he sneered at her. "You have one more chance. You get out there and sign those papers. One more thing goes wrong, and your man is dead. You'll go back to a corpse, you got that?"

She nodded. "I didn't do this on purpose. Please don't hurt him."

"He's already hurt. Don't think I won't tell Jazz to kill him."

"I won't."

He smiled, stood up. "There, that's better. I knew you were all right. Let's go get this paperwork out of the way, then we'll go relax at the beach. How does that sound?"

"Great," she said, struggling to make her voice stop shaking and sound normal.

What she couldn't do was stop the rest of her from shaking. God, how she wanted to, but her body wouldn't obey. Even when they got back to the office where the papers waited in neat order, she couldn't hide the way her hand trembled as she picked up the pen.

"If you'd like to wait until you feel better," the bank executive said, "it's no problem."

She looked at Ed, then at the man. "Mr. Granger, I'm sorry. It's not going to be better later. I'm agoraphobic—do you know what that is?"

"A fear of being in public, yes?"

She nodded. "I know I need to sign these papers in person, but it's difficult for me. I'm just sorry to trouble you with my problems."

"There's no problem at all. In fact, once you've signed at the X's, there's no reason we can't do everything else for you and your uncle. We have his information, and I'll have Joseph give him the new account number right now." Granger picked up the phone.

While he made the arrangements, she signed each line following a red X. Fifty million dollars would be transferred from her account to Ed's, and that would be that. Even if he was convicted of all his crimes, she didn't think the bank could reverse the transfer. It was the Caymans after all, and from their standpoint everything was being done according to the law.

She didn't give a damn about the money, except that it would hurt her father to realize what had happened. He would have given the bastard the fifty million from his own funds given the choice.

As she signed her name for the last time, it was very clear to her that she was signing her death warrant. Michael was hurt. He wasn't going to be able to carry out his part of the plan, and she'd botched her part... What was left but for both of them to die?

All she could hope for at this stage was to stop Michael's pain. If she simply went along with everything Ed said, there was a chance they would be merciful. What a thing to wish for.

"CHRIST, MIKEY, I DON'T want to do this. You know that. You're my brother, for God's sake."

"Then put the gun down."

"I can't." Charlie wiped his nose with the side of his arm. "He'll kill me."

"He" was Jazz, standing in the doorway, his arms folded across his chest, his big teeth shining as he smiled like a child on Christmas morning.

"He'll kill you anyway, you idiot."

"No, no. You don't understand. I brought them this deal. I'm just clearing my debt."

"You know too much, Charlie. They can't let you walk away. What if you decide to blackmail them later?"

"Are you crazy? It's Ed Martini. No one double-crosses Martini."

Michael took one step toward his brother. "That's 'cause no one lives long enough. There's no way you're getting off this boat, Charlie. Not onto dry land."

"Shut up. You think you know so much. You didn't even know I could get into your safe, huh? You didn't know I watched you that night when I was sick. You thought I was sleeping, but I wasn't. I was behind the door and I watched you type in the numbers."

"That was pretty slick, there, Charlie. You sure had me fooled."

"Yeah, I know. You think I'm an idiot, but I'm not. I thought of this whole plan all by myself."

"Dad would be so proud."

Charlie lifted the gun and waved it at Michael's

face. "You don't talk about him. He trusted you. You were supposed to take care of me—and look what you did. You're the reason I got to pull this trigger. It's not my fault."

Michael felt so incredibly tired and he hurt so goddamn much that he almost wanted Charlie to pull the trigger. Only there was someone much more important he had to think about. Besides, he didn't want to give Jazz the satisfaction. "Charlie, put down the gun. I'll get you out of this. Alive."

Jazz laughed, but Charlie didn't see the humor. "You fucking liar. You just want to be with your rich girlfriend. Well, screw you!"

"It's not about her, Charlie. It's about Dad. About the promise I made him. I don't want to hurt you. And I don't want *them* to hurt you."

"I'm the one with the gun."

"You are, but Charlie," he said, his voice growing calm and quiet, "you've never been very good in this kind of situation."

"See? There you go again." He stepped closer and pushed the barrel of the gun into Michael's chest. "I am not an idiot!" he screamed, sending spittle and fear into Michael's face.

"Oh, Charlie," Michael whispered. "I don't know why it had to be so hard for you."

"What?"

"I'm sorry, buddy."

"It's too late now."

"I know, but I'm sorry anyway."

Charlie looked down at the gun, and Michael spun half a step back, then knocked Charlie's feet from underneath him. He grabbed the gun, turning it sideways, and as Charlie fell, Michael put a bullet right into Jazz's chest.

Charlie looked up at him with shock and hurt in his eyes. Michael pointed the weapon at his brother. "I'm sorry," he said again, but this time it was to his father. He fired once more.

"I'M SORRY, MS. BAXTER, there's one more thing we need to complete before we can let you go."

"That's okay," she said, trying not to panic. She looked at Ed and willed him to understand this wasn't her fault.

"What's the hang-up?" he asked.

"In order to transfer this amount of money, Ms. Baxter and you need to fill out statements that will go on record here. As a cooperating member of the international community, we have to have a signed statement that the money will not be used in money-laundering schemes or for any purpose that could be construed as terrorism or supporting known terrorists."

"Sure," Ed said. "We'll sign whatever you like."

"Excellent." He put the papers down in front of them, but Tate noticed there was a slight bulge under hers, toward the bottom. She looked up to find Mr. Granger staring at her. He glanced pointedly at the paper.

She moved the top sheet aside and saw a note in faint script. *Are you in trouble?*

She wanted so badly to say yes. She looked at him again, smiled as earnestly as she knew how and shook her head.

He nodded. She signed. It was over. At least this

part. She still had to make it back to the boat. To find Michael, to help him, no matter what condition he was in. Just thinking about his hands made her sick. What was she going to do if they'd done worse?

AT THE LAST SECOND he moved the gun. The bullet hit inches from Charlie's head.

Michael couldn't stop to figure out why he'd done it. He just had to make sure Charlie didn't call out to Danny or the other one. He dropped to his knees right next to his brother and pulled back his left arm. When Charlie hoisted himself up into the right position, Michael hit him in the temple.

Charlie went down hard. It probably was a good thing Michael's right hand was out of commission. There had been no kidding around with that punch. It was meant to silence. Sometimes it happened that the silence went on forever. He didn't think Charlie was dead and he wasn't going to check. Not right now.

He rose once more and looked at Charlie's gun. It was a Sig Sauer P-226, a gun Michael particularly liked. He had to use his teeth to check the magazine, which was full. He locked the mag back in the gun.

Jazz had fallen in the doorway, and by the time Michael got to him, he must have bled out—if the shot hadn't killed him on impact. Michael had wanted to do him slowly, to make him suffer, but he'd take what he could get. He stepped over the scumbag and went on the prowl.

He wasn't sure how long Ed would keep Tate in the bank, but he wanted everything completed when they returned. Maybe he could take his time with Ed. It would be good to let him know what happened to men who messed with Michael Caulfield's lady. On the other hand, Tate didn't need to have any more trauma in her life. Especially not from him.

No one was in the saloon. But there was someone in the wheelhouse. He was on the radio, and Michael figured he'd better get to him double time. It was the cabin boy, the kid Charlie had lied about. Michael got all the way across the saloon before he turned. The dude had a muscleman's build and a bullfrog's face. He seemed damned surprised to find Michael pointing a gun his way and made a foolish attempt to retrieve his own weapon from his underarm holster.

He fell across the seat, then tumbled to the deck. Michael picked up bullfrog's Walther PPK, but he preferred the Sig. He pulled the magazine out of the Walther and tossed it behind the saloon couch. The gun went into a fake potted plant.

Once he had the Sig in his hand again Michael went looking for Danny. The boat was anchored far from any neighboring vessels. There were people out there, but none of them would have heard the silenced gunshots. He doubted they would hear anything more than innocuous pops if he took a dozen shots off the port bow. It didn't matter. No one was coming to the rescue. It was all on him.

He headed down below. To his right was the galley, and he knew someone was inside from the whistling. "Alouette." He doubted it was Danny. Probably the cook, which sounded innocent enough until you thought about who he cooked for. No one on this boat was without a weapon—that much Michael knew. The cook, despite his ability to make a very excellent salmon steak, wasn't gonna make it.

With his right hand throbbing at nearly his pain threshold, Michael was more than ready to have this over and done with. If it was Danny in the galley, so much the better. If not, he couldn't be far.

Michael inched his way along the teak floor, the incredible interior of the boat showing just how much a bookie like Ed earned for himself. Of course now, with the fifty million in his pocket, he'd probably consider this a toy boat. Something convenient to take him out to his real yacht.

He stopped thinking about Ed. He was all about the whistler in the galley. Whatever the guy was making, there was some chopping involved. That's all that sound could be. So that meant a knife. Not a problem.

Moving as quietly as he could while keeping his balance, Michael made it halfway to the galley. He had to forget about his right hand, about that arm. If he gave it any attention, his instinct would be to pull it from the safety of his back. It was best to concentrate on the gun in his left hand. He listened carefully to the chopping and the whistling, figuring the size of the galley and where his shot should go. There was no room for error, so the second shot had to be close to the first but lower. Get him in the chest, then in the gut. That would take him down without giving him a chance to shoot back.

After a cleansing breath, he got close, a step away. He turned, aimed, adjusted two inches and pulled the trigger. The first bullet threw the cook forward, over his chopped vegetables. The second severed his spinal cord. At least that's what it looked like from the way the man fell.

Michael turned to move deeper into the boat. There should only be one man left on board, not counting Charlie.

Ed was gonna be so pissed.

Michael whistled "Alouette" as he continued the hunt.

THEY WERE OUTSIDE once more, in the bright island sunshine. There were so many people on the streets, mostly tourists with gifts in big bags and flip-flops on their feet. There were more cars now, too. And she wondered how many accidents there were here just because the American tourists had to drive on the left.

Ed had his hand locked on her upper arm, but he seemed a lot happier now that he was so much richer. She felt certain that all he wanted was to get back to the boat, wait till nightfall and make sure there was no one left to tell the tale.

He walked her across the street, making her wait for the light. Then they went toward the beach and the water taxis.

"There's no reason to kill us," she said. "Now that you have the money, there's no way for us to get it back."

"Shut up."

"Just let us go. We'll disappear. You won't hear from us again."

"I said shut up."

She did, but with every step her worry grew, and she kept picturing horror after horror of what she'd find on the boat. It was making it hard to see, hard to breathe, but she didn't want to worry Michael by showing up in a full-blown panic attack.

"Come on," Ed said, squeezing her arm.

"You're hurting me."

"Just get your ass in gear. I want to get back to the boat. We're celebrating tonight at the Ritz. Figure I'm gonna buy myself one hell of an expensive bottle of champagne." He tugged her again, practically pulling her shoulder out of its socket.

She stopped and tore her arm free, suddenly so filled with rage she forgot all about her constricted breath and pounding heartbeat.

He was celebrating at the Ritz? Over his dead body.

# 18

"I DON'T CARE WHAT evidence you have or don't have. I know Michael Caulfield is behind this."

Sara bit her lower lip, trying hard not to react. Mr. Baxter needed to have his say. She turned to Special Agent Webber and he gave her a small nod. They'd talked a lot yesterday, after she'd cried her millionth tear.

She'd recognized Tate's purse instantly. That the wallet was still inside shut down the last of her hope. It didn't matter that the money was gone. Tate wouldn't have left that wallet. It had been a gift. From Sara.

She'd debated long and hard about telling William about the purse, but in the end she'd decided he had to know. There was no choice.

He'd disappeared into the guest room, then emerged this morning more angry than sad. He'd called the meeting they were having now. Who knows? His righteous anger just might pull him through.

"Sir, we're doing everything we can to find both your daughter and Mr. Caulfield. We know his motorcycle is missing, but from the state of his apartment it doesn't appear he planned a trip. There were no suitcases missing, all his clothing was in the drawers and closets. Frankly we're much more interested in Jerry Brody than Caulfield."

"*I'm* interested in Caulfield. He was in military intelligence. I doubt very much he intended anyone to think he'd planned this. I didn't hire him because he was a fool."

"I understand, sir. Rest assured, we're leaving no stone unturned. We're currently investigating his brother, where there might be some connection."

"His brother."

"Charles. He has a criminal record. Theft, racketeering, drugs."

William stood so quickly he had to grab the edge of his chair to gain his balance. "I knew it. That's why they needed the five million—drug money."

"Mr. Baxter," Sara said, concerned now that he was working himself into such a lather. "I know it seems to make sense that Michael was in on this, but—"

"Enough," he said.

He'd never raised his voice at her before, and she didn't much care for it now. But the man was given a pass, at least for today.

"I know what I know."

"Excuse me, Mr. Baxter?"

Sara, as well as the men in the room, all turned as one to see three of the security team standing by the side wall. They all looked uncomfortable, as if they had thrown a baseball through a stained-glass window.

"Who are you?" Baxter asked.

The tallest one stepped forward. "I'm George Bryan. I work surveillance."

"I'm E. J. Packer, sir." Sara recognized him from

the scars on his face. "I'm ex-Army intelligence and I run night security."

They both turned to the only blond, a slender man with horn-rimmed glasses. "I'm also ex-Army intelligence, sir. Name's McPherson. Bill McPherson."

"What is it?"

"I served with Mike Caulfield for two years. He is not your man."

"What?" William looked from the men to Sara, as if she'd been behind this mutiny.

"I also served with Mike Caulfield." This from George Bryan. "I can't see it, Mr. Baxter. If he's involved, it's because he's trying to save her. I've never worked for a more honorable man."

"I agree, Mr. Baxter." E.J. nodded toward Sara. "Ma'am. For my money, looking at Caulfield is looking in the wrong direction."

"Get out of here, all of you," Baxter said, his face red with rage. "You work for him. Of course you're going to say he's innocent."

The three men, all with their military stance and utmost respect, took his fury like good soldiers. And when they were summarily fired, they didn't seem surprised.

But when Sara looked back at the FBI agent, it was clear attention had been paid.

"YOU SON OF A BITCH!" Tate said so loudly the tourists in back of Ed stopped talking to stare. "You murdering bastard. You're planning on killing us before you have your champagne?"

He laughed as he looked around nervously. With his

left hand he pulled out his cell phone. "I'm warning you," he said, his teeth clamped together as he smiled.

"You're warning me…what? That you're going to hurt Michael? You're planning to kill us. What could hurt worse than that?"

"Stop it," he said. "These people are going to think you're serious."

She was serious. So serious that she didn't even stop to think, she just turned in front of him, grabbed his arms and kneed Ed Martini right between the legs.

He howled so loudly everyone on the street stopped, and when he fell to the ground, clutching his crotch, more and more people approached. But Tate wasn't done yet.

She circled around to his back. His piteous cries had the crowd murmuring, but she didn't care. She lifted his Hawaiian shirt above his waist and plucked the gun away.

Several members of the crowd backed up. Despite the hysteria she felt just under the surface, the gun in Tate's hands didn't shake at all. She moved around in front of the man and kept the barrel pointed at his head. "Someone call the cops."

She didn't hear any movement. "Someone," she said again, only a whole lot louder, "call the cops."

There were footsteps to her right and in back of her. Horns honked in the road, and she assumed the crowd had gotten so large that they were blocking the street. Hell, they probably didn't see a sight like this every day.

Ed Martini writhed on the sidewalk, holding himself like a child who has to pee. Martini, who hadn't blinked when Michael's wrist had been broken, who thought nothing of killing two innocent people, then drinking champagne. The pig deserved to die himself, but maybe it would be worse for him if he had to go to prison here. She didn't think the Caymans had extradition laws, but that didn't matter either. He wasn't going to kill Michael. Not now.

"Hey, hey. Put the gun down, miss."

She looked up to see two police officers standing on the road. "He's a kidnapper and a thief and a murderer, and I have proof of all of it."

"Put the gun down and we'll talk."

She didn't want to. She wanted to pull the trigger. But she didn't. She just bent, put the gun on the ground and backed away.

The cops, in their crisp khakis and black hats, split up, with one man shooing the bystanders away and the other coming toward her. Two steps in, Ed lunged forward and grabbed the gun.

She leaped back, cursing herself for not kicking the weapon as far as she could.

Ed got to his knees, then to his feet, the gun in his right hand pointing at her chest. His face was a red mess, with tears and more dripping from his nose and chin. He didn't look so smooth now. What he did look like was a man who didn't care about consequences. Not when he clearly wanted to kill her so damn badly.

"Sir, put the gun down. Sir…"

Ed didn't even glance at the cop. He just snarled at Tate. "You bitch. You're gonna pay—"

"I've already paid. Isn't fifty-five million enough? Isn't kidnapping and assault enough? You broke his wrists! All he was trying to do was protect me, and you've crippled him."

"He's long past caring," he said, lifting the gun. "And in one second you're going to be, too."

Tate closed her eyes, prepared for the impact of a bullet to send her crashing into the crowd. But it didn't come. She heard a scuffle, then a thunk, and she opened her eyes to see the two sturdy police officers on top of Ed, their knees planted on his back as they twisted his hands around for cuffs.

Tears filled her eyes and she laughed and wept as she realized it was over, that Ed was really in custody. And then it hit her, what he'd said about Michael.

Her legs didn't want to hold her up as she let the truth in. Michael was dead. They hadn't broken his other wrist, they'd shot him. Of course they had. Why bother to keep him around? She'd proved she would do anything for him, so all they'd needed was her own belief that she could save him.

Michael was dead.

LEAVING THE COOK IN the galley, Michael went back down the narrow corridor toward the master suite and the other berth. Danny, unless he'd taken Ed and Tate to the island, had to be there somewhere. Probably prepared, as the cook's death hadn't been all that quiet.

There was a head just before the smaller berth, and Michael slowed as he neared it. His arm and shoulder throbbed to the beat of his heart as he silently made his approach.

Gun at the ready, he kicked the door in, but no one was there. The room was too small to hide in, which meant Danny had to be in one of the bedrooms. If he was on board at all.

The berth, with a couple of beds and very little else, did have space to hide. Although a man Danny's size would have trouble.

If the roles had been reversed, Michael would have gotten behind the door, listening carefully for footsteps. He wouldn't wait for his assailant to show up, he'd shoot through the door.

With that in mind, Michael decided to lure Danny out. He still had a lot of ammo in the mag, so he got close, aimed his weapon at the master suite door and fired.

Despite the name, silencers never really silenced a gun. They helped, but for anyone below deck, the gunshot would have been heard. Just in case Danny had headphones on, Michael put the gun under his right armpit—which hurt like a bitch—unscrewed the silencer, then retrieved the weapon. Two more shots, and this time someone would have to be dead to miss the sound.

Michael crouched in the head doorway, waiting. It was tough to be patient. His mind went one of two places—Tate or pain. He had to keep bringing himself back to his target.

Three minutes went by and Michael saw the door to the master suite move.

Danny had ducked—at least that's what it looked like from the position of his gun. It didn't matter. He could have crawled out on his belly. For all his size and weight, there was nothing the man could have done to save his own life.

Michael put three shots into the door. Danny fell like a massive tree, his head cracking loudly on the teak floor.

Michael backed up until he could sit on the edge of the john. His whole body throbbed with pain, mitigated slightly by relief. Even that only lasted a minute. Tate was still out there. And Charlie.

He hadn't heard a thing from upstairs, but that didn't mean Charlie hadn't recovered. At least his brother didn't have a gun. He'd probably end up shooting himself if he had.

Michael stood, momentarily dizzy. Then, after a few deep breaths, he headed back to the saloon. The smell of death followed him, tainting the scent of the ocean. He felt pretty sure that the coppery taste at the back of his mouth would remind him of tropical islands for some time to come.

The saloon itself was in good shape. Michael's gaze went right to the big leather chair. The government would be selling off the boat once Ed was in prison, and it felt damn good to know the bastard would never sit in that chair again.

Michael needed Tate to get back. Looking toward the beach, he didn't see any water taxis—but then, they were pretty far offshore.

Shit, he couldn't put it off any longer. He turned to the small room that had been their prison for ten days. Jazz's body was still in the doorway, and beyond him, Charlie.

IT HAD TAKEN TOO LONG for the police to get their act together once the street cops had taken her to the station. She'd had to scream to get the right person's attention, but once Chief Eccles understood what was at stake, he made things happen.

In fact, she had to fill in the details as they sped to

a police boat. It was long and sleek and, according to the chief, faster than the speed of criminals.

He brought along six men, heavily armed, in what she assumed to be the British colonial equivalent of a SWAT team. As they flew over the water toward the *Pretty Kitty,* all Tate could do was pray. If only he could still be alive, she'd give more money to charity. She'd work in a soup kitchen. She'd trade years off her own life. Anything. Just not what Ed had said. Not that.

She stood up, too insane to be still, next to the captain. Wind and sea mist sprayed her face, ruining the makeup she'd so carefully applied this morning. Well, that and her tears.

CHARLIE HADN'T MOVED at all, and as Michael knelt next to him, his chest constricted with a stab of guilt and regret. He put his fingers to Charlie's throat, searching for a pulse. He thought maybe…but that could be his own heartbeat.

He bent down, putting his ear right over Charlie's heart. There, damn it. He wasn't dead. He wasn't in great shape, but he wasn't dead.

Relief made his eyes water as he sat back up. Now it was just a matter of time before Tate and Ed came back. Before Michael could finish taking the trash out.

He put his left hand down to steady himself as he rose.

The blow to the back of his head pitched him forward again, and for a second he thought Ed had returned to surprise him. But when he looked up, it wasn't Ed but the not-so-dead, very pissed off Jazz.

THERE IT WAS IN THE distance, the *Pretty Kitty*. She'd been brought aboard unconscious and she'd been taken under duress, so this was the first time Tate had really seen the boat. It was gorgeous. Sleek like a cheetah, it was an exceptional yacht in a harbor full of yachts. No wonder they'd gotten to the Caymans so quickly.

The beauty of the vessel paled as the thought occurred again, as fresh as the first time, that it was Michael's coffin. She chased the image away as quickly as it had come, but there was no more admiration for the boat.

She held on to the dash, willing this boat to hurry. To take her to the man she loved. To find him alive. Nothing else mattered. Nothing.

JAZZ STOOD UNSTEADILY on his widespread legs. His shirt—Hawaiian, like Ed's—was matted with blood. Blood that dripped down his fingers into the pale plush carpet.

He glowered at Michael with malevolent red eyes. "You're gonna die," he said. "You are gonna die slow."

Michael reached for his weapon, stuck into the folds of his pillowcase brace, but Jazz beat him to the punch with his own second gun at the small of his back. The Derringer was small, but it would kill just fine.

"Drop it," Jazz said.

"Like hell. It's over, Jazz. You're the only one left alive."

"Ed's still alive."

"He won't be—"

Charlie moaned. Of all the rotten timing… He moaned again and moved his head.

Jazz sneered and moved his gun so it pointed at Charlie. "You still think you can stop me?"

Michael smiled as he got to his feet. "With one hand tied behind my back, asshole."

Jazz took a step back, a hell of a lot more shaken than he'd been a minute ago. "Stop there or I kill him."

"Go ahead," Michael said. "You pull that trigger, it's the last thing you ever do."

"Fuck you, man." He jerked the gun up to shoot, but Michael was quicker. He dived over Charlie, knocking Jazz off his feet. Jazz lost his gun, but he still had his hands and he hit Michael, hard, in the right shoulder. The pain nearly knocked him out, but not quite.

The second blow hit his bad shoulder again. Michael had to get his left hand moving. He had to get his gun up, aimed at Jazz—and this time there could be no mistakes.

He could feel Jazz's knee come up against his stomach, his fist come down on his shoulder, then his other fist into his head. It was the most inelegant fight Michael had ever seen, but it was working. In another minute Jazz would be out from under him, and once that happened, adrenaline alone would carry him through.

With all the energy he had left in his body Michael pulled his left arm up, raised it above his head, stuck the barrel in Jazz's gut.

He almost lost it as Jazz bellowed and struck him fiercely in the head, in the shoulder, in the stomach. But Jazz didn't hit him in the left hand.

Michael pulled the trigger.

The sound of the gunshot filled his head as blood splattered his body.

He tried to move, to get off the dead man, but all his strength had gone with that last bullet.

He felt the dark close in on him. And he felt grateful.

"You have to stay here."

"I can't."

Chief Eccles shook his head, even as he braced himself as the grappling hooks pulled the police boat up against the *Pretty Kitty*. "We don't have any idea who's up there and how many weapons are on board. You could be killed."

"I don't care. If Michael is alive, he'll need me."

"The ambulance boat will be here in a moment."

"Please," she begged. "I have to—"

"I know you want to see him. But I can't let you on board. I promise I'll let you see him as soon as it's safe."

She couldn't argue anymore. They were in position and ready to board. Numbly she watched as the men in their heavy armor climbed up into the yacht, quickly disappearing into the saloon.

She'd given the chief Michael's description, afraid that they'd think he was one of Ed's men. Even so, the thought scared her. Maybe scared was better than knowing. She could deal with scared.

The minutes ticked by. She heard no gunfire. There were shouts, but she couldn't understand the words. The ambulance boat pulled up, and as quickly as they could the EMTs climbed into the yacht, carrying heavy bags and a portable gurney.

If they could go aboard, that must mean that the

coast was clear, right? What kind of chief would let his EMTs walk into a gun battle?

There was only one cop left on the police boat. His job was probably to keep her from disembarking, but at the moment he was busy on the radio, his gaze on the ambulance boat.

That was all the permission she needed. With strength she didn't know she had, she jumped over to the ladder leading up to the *Pretty Kitty*'s saloon. She made it onto the yacht just as the cop assigned to watch her shouted out. But he was too late—she was going to find Michael no matter what.

There was a huddle of men just at the door to their room. EMTs crouched beside someone, but she couldn't see who.

She took one step, then another, dread and hope battling it out in her head. When she saw them lift Michael's body onto the gurney, her heart shattered.

She was too late. Ed had told her the truth. Michael—her lover, her hero, her friend—was dead.

They came toward her, one EMT pushing the gurney and Michael. Her horrified gaze took in all the blood, all the bruises on Michael's face. God, they'd tortured him. Tortured him, then killed him in cold blood.

"Miss?"

She looked up into the dark man's face.

"Why don't you come with us? I'm sure he'll feel better seeing you first thing when he wakes up."

Tate blinked. "What?"

"I said why don't you come with us?"

"No—that last part. You said when he wakes up?"

The EMT nodded. "He's gonna be sore as heck, but he'll be fine."

The words took their own sweet time sinking in. And when they did, when she finally got that she hadn't lost him after all, Tate fainted dead away.

# 19

THE PHONE RANG AT eight-forty, stopping Sara just as she was about to leave Tate's place. The day had been so horrible, starting with that dreadful meeting first thing, that she'd made an appointment to get a deep-tissue massage to work out some of her stress.

She turned, going toward the nearest phone, but William beat her to it. She smiled at him, then went back to the door. When he gasped, she stopped.

"My God, my God, it's really you!"

Sara's heart slammed into overdrive as she hurried back to the phone. She dropped her tote and held on to the living room wall as the truth sunk in. Even if there had been no words spoken, she would have known it was Tate by looking at William. He was pale as a ghost, far too thin and haggard, but the joy in his eyes was like a rebirth.

"Where?"

Sara wanted desperately to hear Tate's voice. She knew it was real, but she still needed more.

"I'll be there by morning. You don't worry about a thing. I'll come get you and we'll straighten everything out."

Sara watched as fat tears slid down the old man's

cheeks. Her own tears started then, and her chest got tight with a mixture of emotions too big to hold in.

"Yes, she's here. She's been here the whole time. She'll come with me."

Sara nodded happily, wondering a million things at once.

William's face changed and so did his posture. "We'll talk about him when I get there."

Michael. It had to be. Oh, thank God. He must be alive, too, and they'd been together. Finally the whole story would come out. Jerry Brody, the main suspect, had sworn the kidnapping had nothing to do with him, but now everyone would find out for sure.

She didn't care. Tate was alive. For the first time in ten days Sara could breathe.

When Mr. Baxter hung up, he grabbed her in a hug that would leave bruises tomorrow. It was perfect.

"YOU'RE UP."

Michael turned at the sound of Tate's voice to find her sitting beside his bed. His hospital bed. "How'd I get here?"

"The cavalry showed up. Too late to be of much help to you, however."

"Doesn't matter. You're here."

She smiled, wishing now that she'd had a few more moments with a hairbrush and some makeup. She'd done little but cry since she'd been roused on the ambulance boat. Michael had still not gained consciousness at the time, and as she'd waved away the concerned medics, she'd asked them a hundred questions—all of them nonsense, really, because Michael was alive.

She'd ridden with him to the hospital, and while he'd had his wrist worked on she'd called her father. It had been so good to speak to him, to know that Sara was there and that she'd taken care of him. They would all be together in the morning, which was wonderful, but right now she needed to be with Michael. To make sure he was all right and that he wasn't going to disappear.

"How long have I been out of it?"

"It's ten. At night, just so we're clear."

He looked at his bandaged hand. "Is this all the damage?"

"To you, yes."

"They found all the bodies?"

She nodded. "There's going to be an inquest, but don't worry. You'll be cleared in a moment. Ed's in jail and he's not ever getting out."

"Charlie?"

"He'll live. He's here in the hospital. He has a concussion, that's all. But I'm afraid he won't be getting off so easily."

Michael looked away. "I'm glad he didn't die."

She scooted her chair closer to the bed and touched his arm. "I called my father. He and Sara are flying in first thing in the morning."

"Good. Great."

"You'll be released by then. But I'm afraid you'll be in police custody until the inquest. I was assured there would be no delay. When my father gets here—"

"I'll hand in my resignation."

"I was going to say he'll make sure you'll have everything you need. I've gotten us a room at the Ritz, so as soon as you're free—"

"Tate... I appreciate all of this. I do. But let's slow down a little. There's a lot to deal with, and my head's still too fuzzy to understand it all."

"Of course," she said, embarrassed at her own presumption. "I'll call the nurse."

"Thanks," he said. "I'm probably going to be knocked out till morning. I'll sleep better knowing you're getting some rest."

"I'm fine. That chair is really comfortable."

He shook his head. "Go to the hotel," he said too quietly. "Get a good night's sleep. We'll talk tomorrow."

His tone was gentle and concerned, but his message burned in her chest. He wanted her gone. What she didn't know was if he meant for tonight or forever.

Frankly she wasn't in any shape to ask the question. Better to leave it unanswered than to know for sure. "Okay. I'll send the nurse."

Michael nodded. His gorgeous face looked even more rugged with the dark bruises and his five-o'clock shadow. She hated that he'd been so badly hurt, but her prayers had been answered. He was alive. It shouldn't matter that he was sending her away. It shouldn't—but it did.

She stood, put the chair back, then headed for the door.

"Tate?"

She stopped.

"No kiss goodbye?"

She smiled as she went back to him. She bent over him and brushed her lips over his. He touched her arm with his left hand as he kissed her back.

When she pulled away, the look in his eyes told her everything. When he'd asked for a kiss goodbye, he'd meant it.

THE JET TOUCHED DOWN at seven-eighteen Caymans time. Tate had gotten to the airport forty minutes earlier and had too many cups of coffee as she'd waited.

The good night's sleep she'd promised Michael hadn't materialized. She'd lain awake in her very posh suite, thinking. The fact that she'd still felt as if she was rocking on the water didn't help, either, but mostly she'd just thought.

She'd wanted a kidnapping to change her life and she'd gotten what she'd asked for. She hadn't bargained on the close calls with death. But then, she hadn't bargained on Michael, either.

Bottom line, however, was that she would never be the same.

She'd faced off with Ed, and despite his gun and his cell phone, she'd come out the victor. She'd kicked her kidnapper's ass. That wasn't opinion, it was fact.

Would she ever have another panic attack? Yeah, probably. There had been that whole passing-out business when she'd found out Michael was alive. But the good news was she wasn't going to stop living. She wasn't going to hole herself up in her luxurious prison of a penthouse. She was a free woman. Forever more, if she did have a panic attack, she could think of the satisfying crunch of Ed's testicles against her kneecap. That would surely get her through.

The bigger question was what she was going to do about Michael.

There was no doubt in her mind that she loved him. That she wanted to be with him, and not just for a fling. But she also wasn't naive enough to think that scenario wasn't rife with problems. There was her father to deal with. And the money thing. Then there was his guilt about his brother. None of those issues was going to be worked out with a nice chat.

She was, however, not willing to let him go just because she wasn't sure about how things would work. They'd just have to take it one step at a time.

Assuming, of course, he was willing to try.

The glass door between the tarmac and the terminal slid open, and there was her father.

She ran to him and gave him a hug he'd never forget. Fresh tears came from that never-ending supply, but these were joyous, so maybe they didn't count.

He petted her head as he rocked her back and forth. She felt like a little girl again, safe in her daddy's arms.

Finally she pulled back, kissed him on the cheek, then jumped into another fierce round of hugs with Sara.

It took a while, but they all finally finished crying and hugging and went off to the hotel.

She talked the entire way, and after they'd checked in, she continued the tale in her father's suite. She emphasized that Michael had saved her life many times over, but her father could be the most stubborn man.

"Don't get me wrong—I'm grateful he saved your life. But if it wasn't for him, you wouldn't have been in that position in the first place."

"Stop," she said. "I know you want someone to

blame, so here's a really good solution. Blame Ed Martini. He's the one who kidnapped me, who threatened me. He was going to kill me that first night, after he got the ransom. Then he was going to kill me as soon as he got the big money. He tried to kill me in the middle of the street in George Town. That's who you can blame. And when you're done with that, you can go to Michael Caulfield and you can thank him for your daughter's life."

Her father looked at her for a long time, and while a stranger would have thought he was completely unmoved by her speech, she knew he had listened. More importantly, he'd heard.

"You care about him," Sara said.

She looked at her oldest friend. "I do."

"Is he really going to resign?"

"I believe he is."

"And?"

Tate sighed. There was no time like the present to let her father know exactly where she stood. "I don't know. I need to make some phone calls. Michael needs an attorney and I want to make sure the inquest is in motion."

She kissed her father on the cheek, did the same to Sara, then went for the door. "Get unpacked," she said, standing in the doorway. "I'm in 2720. I'd appreciate any help you two want to give me."

With that, she left the suite. On the one hand, she'd said what she needed to and felt stronger than ever. On the other hand, she was scared beyond words that Michael would disappear before she had a chance to figure out what to do.

MICHAEL SAT IN THE beach chair, staring out at the ocean as the sun rose in splendor. This was the fifth morning in a row he'd come out for the sunrise, coffee in hand—left hand—the day stretching achingly ahead of him.

He'd found this little bungalow a week ago, after all the legal maneuverings had ended and he was once again a free man. After he'd said goodbye to Tate.

Charlie was in prison, and Michael doubted he'd ever be released. It was hard justice, but there was nothing Michael could do to mitigate the circumstances. Charlie had made his bed. Michael supposed he'd feel guilty about it for the rest of his life—but then, that was *his* bed. His very lonely bed.

His hand was healing and his bruises were all but gone, but he couldn't stop thinking about Tate. She'd sounded completely convincing when she'd asked him to come back. To try and live a life with her. But he knew the score. Despite his thanks, he knew William blamed him. Hell, he still blamed himself. As for a life with Tate? She was just starting to live. She deserved the world, not him. God, not him.

Sara had come in to double-team him. But at least she'd understood when Michael had explained. Tate still would have none of it.

After many tears and a lot of heartache for both of them, she'd gotten on her father's private plane and gone back to New York.

So here he was, sitting on a beach, sipping coffee, unsure what he was going to do with the day, not to mention the rest of his life. Missing Tate Baxter more than he'd ever imagined. More than he could take.

TATE STARED AT THE foolish trompe l'oeil window in her bedroom. It symbolized so much. Her pretense of a life. Her false dreams of adventure and romance. Every precious moment she'd wasted in her fear.

She owed Dr. Bay an apology. In retrospect, the kidnapping had been a good idea—the fake kind, at least. Tate truly was a different woman now. Yes, she still suffered from nightmares and she wasn't going to give up on therapy anytime soon, but she no longer wanted to hide herself away. Life beckoned in the most alluring ways. Unfortunately her new dreams all centered around a man who didn't want her.

It occurred to her that she might not be thinking in the most rational terms. The experiences on the boat had been traumatic and profound. Perhaps, as her father had suggested, she'd gone through some sort or variation of Stockholm syndrome, where her beliefs about Michael were totally out of proportion to actual events.

But after a month back home of intensive journaling and visits to her new therapist, she didn't think so.

She missed him. So badly it ached, and not in a metaphorical sense. She yearned to be with him, to hear his voice, smell his scent. She couldn't stand that he was alone, that his hand wouldn't heal for a while yet, that he had to deal with the consequences of his brother's sentence. All alone. He'd put his own life at risk so many times for her. But it wasn't just gratitude or guilt that made her want him.

She'd become someone new with him. She'd seen herself through his eyes, and for the first time in her life she'd liked what she'd seen.

Michael believed in her. He'd convinced her of her own strength over and over again.

And, she had to admit, she missed making love to him. There was no doubt in her mind that the two of them were meant to be together.

Unfortunately there was a giant roadblock between them, and it wasn't the fact that he blamed himself for the kidnapping. It was the money.

"Knock-knock."

Tate turned to find Sara at the bedroom door. "I'm so glad you're here."

"Right back at ya," Sara said. She was in her workout gear, looking radiant, and she sat on the bed with a plop. "Come with me?"

"I will," Tate said. "But not today."

"You said that yesterday. I know you'll like my trainer. He's got the best ass in the five boroughs. Seriously. It's worth all the pain just to watch him bend over."

Tate grinned. "I missed you."

"I'm glad. It would have hurt my feelings if you hadn't."

"You're my sister, kiddo. So when I ask you something, I trust you're going to be honest, right?"

Sara crossed her heart.

"I can't let go of Michael. I miss him too much. I love him."

Sara's smile faded as she nodded. "I figured."

"I want to go to him. Do whatever it takes to make him see that we can be together. Except...there's the whole money problem."

Sara's head went down for a long time. Tate thought

of calling the kitchen for tea, but she didn't want to disturb Sara's thought process.

Finally her friend looked up. "It's a big problem, and I don't know Michael well enough to predict if he can get past it. But something that might help is the reward."

"What reward?"

"Your father offered a million dollars to anyone who was instrumental in finding you. Michael was instrumental, all right."

"He didn't tell me."

"Yeah," Sara said. "Go figure."

"Surely he'd have to agree that Michael deserves the reward."

Sara laughed. "Your father? Come on, Tate. He's going to blame Michael for a long time."

"But Michael deserves—oh."

"Exactly."

Tate grinned. "Do you think I'm crazy?"

"Only if you don't try. Tate, you haven't taken a risk in so long. I think taking this one will make up for it. The worst that's going to happen is he'll break your heart. And since your heart is already broken, it can't be that much worse."

Tate felt her pulse race and her heart pound. Sara was right. It would be scary to go to him—but then, she had faced scary. And she'd kicked scary's ass.

ANOTHER DAY, ANOTHER sunrise, and Michael wasn't getting better. His hand was healing, but missing Tate continued to get worse.

He didn't understand. Yes, he was depressed. He got

that. He'd made some big mistakes and there had been consequences. That wasn't what was making him nuts.

That had everything to do with Tate. Not Charlie, not the kidnapping, not the killings. Tate haunted his dreams, haunted his waking hours. He kept thinking about how she'd been so brave, how she'd fought so hard. He remembered, too vividly, the way her skin felt, the taste of her flesh, how he felt when he slipped inside her.

He took a sip of coffee, wishing she were there, wishing he could find a way to justify calling her. If he couldn't do that, he wanted a way to forget her. Perhaps now that Charlie was in jail he could go back to the Army. If his hand healed correctly. If they'd take him.

It would all be a lot easier if he would stop thinking he saw her out of the corner of his eye. Every woman with reddish-brown hair made his pulse race. Until he saw that it was just a woman and not Tate. Then he'd hear a voice, and the cycle would start over again until he saw it was a stranger.

The persistence of her memory had taken him over. Like a virus, she had spread throughout his system. Unfortunately there were no pills or shots to help him.

He felt someone next to his chair, but he didn't want any more coffee or a drink. He looked up, ready to send the boy away. But it wasn't a boy. And it wasn't a dream.

"Tate?"

She was wearing shorts and a T-shirt, with her hair down and wild, the way it had been on the boat. She wore no makeup and her eyes were puffy from crying. He'd never seen anyone more beautiful in his life.

"I tried, Michael. I did. I tried to see it your way and

I gave your argument all I could. But the only conclusion I could come to was that you couldn't be more wrong if you tried."

He couldn't help laughing at that, even though she looked damn serious.

"Don't laugh. I mean it. You're an idiot."

"I never had any doubts about that."

"Good, so we're agreed. And since you're an idiot and I'm tough and smart, here's what we're gonna do." She came around in front of him and pulled him up by his T-shirt. "We're going to figure out who we are and what we want and we're going to do it together. I have no idea if it's going to last a week or a lifetime, but I'll be damned if I walk away and don't find out."

"Really?"

"Yes. Any questions?"

"What about your—"

She put her fingers over his mouth. "This isn't about my father. So no questions about him. And it's not about money, because there was a million-dollar reward for my safe return, which you completely and utterly deserve, so you have money, I have money— and, dammit, money isn't the issue."

"Are you through?"

"No. I also want you to know that just because you saved my life doesn't mean I feel some kind of obligation toward you. I'm not going through a phase and I'm not here because you're the first man in years to make my toes curl. I'm here because being with you is the best thing that's happened to me. Ever. You're an amazing man and I admire every single thing about you. Of course, when we actually live together, I reserve the right to get cranky. But still, I think you're incredible and I don't want to spend another day without you."

"Are you through now?"

"For the moment."

"Good. Because I love you."

Her lips curved up in a wicked smile. "Yeah?"

"Yeah."

"All that other stuff?"

He shrugged. "We'll deal."

"I thought this would be harder."

He shook his head. "I can't get you out of my head. You've been driving me insane."

She sighed and closed her eyes. "Thank God. Because I love you, too."

He smiled as his whole body relaxed. "Thank God," he said. And then he kissed her.

\* \* \* \* \*

*For a sneak preview of Marie Ferrarella's
DOCTOR IN THE HOUSE,
coming to NEXT in September,
please turn the page.*

**He** didn't look like an unholy terror.

But maybe that reputation was exaggerated, Bailey DelMonico thought as she turned in her chair to look toward the doorway.

The man didn't seem scary at all.

Dr. Munro, or Ivan the Terrible, was tall, with an athletic build and wide shoulders. The cheekbones beneath what she estimated to be day-old stubble were prominent. His hair was light brown and just this side of unruly. Munro's hair looked as if he used his fingers for a comb and didn't care who knew it.

The eyes were brown, almost black as they were aimed at her. There was no other word for it. Aimed. As if he was debating whether or not to fire at point-blank range.

Somewhere in the back of her mind, a line from a B movie, "Be afraid—be very afraid…" whispered along the perimeter of her brain. Warning her. Almost against her will, it caused her to brace her shoulders. Bailey had to remind herself to breathe in and out like a normal person.

The chief of staff, Dr. Bennett, had tried his level best to put her at ease and had almost succeeded. But an air of tension had entered with Munro. She wondered if Dr. Bennett was bracing himself as well, bracing for some kind of disaster or explosion.

"Ah, here he is now," Harold Bennett announced needlessly. The smile on his lips was slightly forced, and the look in his gray, kindly eyes held a warning as he looked at his chief neurosurgeon. "We were just talking about you, Dr. Munro."

"Can't imagine why," Ivan replied dryly.

Harold cleared his throat, as if that would cover the less than friendly tone of voice Ivan had just displayed. "Dr. Munro, this is the young woman I was telling you about yesterday."

Now his eyes dissected her. Bailey felt as if she was undergoing a scalpel-less autopsy right then and there. "Ah yes, the Stanford Special."

He made her sound like something that was listed at the top of a third-rate diner menu. There was enough contempt in his voice to offend an entire delegation from the UN.

Summoning the bravado that her parents always claimed had been infused in her since the moment she first drew breath, Bailey put out her hand. "Hello. I'm Dr. Bailey DelMonico."

Ivan made no effort to take the hand offered to him. Instead, he slid his long, lanky form bonelessly into the chair beside her. He proceeded to move the chair ever so slightly so that there was even more space between them. Ivan faced the chief of staff, but the words he spoke were addressed to her.

"You're a doctor, DelMonico, when I say you're a

doctor," he informed her coldly, sparing her only one frosty glance to punctuate the end of his statement.

Harold stifled a sigh. "Dr. Munro is going to take over your education. Dr. Munro—" he fixed Ivan with a steely gaze that had been known to send lesser doctors running for their antacids, but, as always, seemed to have no effect on the chief neurosurgeon "—I want you to award her every consideration. From now on, Dr. DelMonico is to be your shadow, your sponge and your assistant." He emphasized the last word as his eyes locked with Ivan's. "Do I make myself clear?"

For his part, Ivan seemed completely unfazed. He merely nodded, his eyes and expression unreadable. "Perfectly."

His hand was on the doorknob. Bailey sprang to her feet. Her chair made a scraping noise as she moved it back and then quickly joined the neurosurgeon before he could leave the office.

Closing the door behind him, Ivan leaned over and whispered into her ear, "Just so you know, I'm going to be your worst nightmare."

Bailey DelMonico has finally
gotten her life on track, and is
passionate about her recent career
change. Nothing will stand in the way
of her becoming a doctor...that is,
until she's paired with the sharp-tongued
Dr. Ivan Munro.

Watch the sparks fly in

# Doctor in
# the House

by *USA TODAY* Bestselling Author

# Marie Ferrarella

Available September 2007

Intrigued? Read more at
**TheNextNovel.com**

## HARLEQUIN *Romance*®

*New York Times* bestselling author

# DIANA PALMER

Handsome, eligible ranch owner Stuart York knew Ivy Conley was too young for him, so he closed his heart to her and sent her away—despite the fireworks between them. Now, years later, Ivy is determined not to be treated like a little girl anymore…but for some reason, Stuart is always fighting her battles for her. And safe in Stuart's arms makes Ivy feel like a woman…his woman.

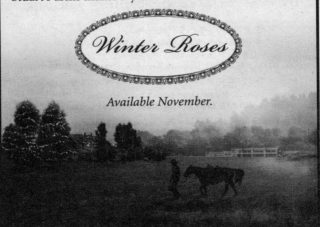

*Winter Roses*

*Available November.*

HRIBC03985

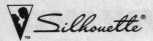

## Silhouette®

### Romantic
# SUSPENSE

**Sparked by Danger,
Fueled by Passion.**

When evidence is found that Mallory Dawes
intends to sell the personal financial information
of government employees to "the Russian,"
OMEGA engages undercover agent Cutter Smith.
Tailing her all the way to France, Cutter is
fighting a growing attraction to Mallory while at
the same time having to determine her connection
to "the Russian." Is Mallory really the mouse in
this game of cat and mouse?

**Look for**

# *Stranded with a Spy*

### by *USA TODAY* bestselling author
# Merline Lovelace
### *October 2007.*

Also available October wherever you buy books:
BULLETPROOF MARRIAGE *(Mission: Impassioned)*
by Karen Whiddon
A HERO'S REDEMPTION *(Haven)* by Suzanne McMinn
TOUCHED BY FIRE by Elizabeth Sinclair

# nocturne™

### Look for
## NIGHT MISCHIEF
### by
# NINA BRUHNS

Lady Dawn Maybank's worst nightmare
is realized when she accidentally conjures
a demon of vengeance, Galen McManus. What
she doesn't realize is that Galen plans to teach
her a lesson in love—one she'll never forget....

# DARK
## ENCHANTMENTS

*Available October wherever you buy books.*

*Don't miss the last installment of Dark Enchantments,*
*SAVING DESTINY by Pat White, available November.*

**HARLEQUIN®**

*Mediterranean* NIGHTS™

*Sail aboard the luxurious Alexandra's Dream and experience glamour, romance, mystery and revenge!*

**Coming in October 2007...**

# AN AFFAIR TO REMEMBER

*by*

*Karen Kendall*

When Captain Nikolas Pappas first fell in love with Helena Stamos, he was a penniless deckhand and she was the daughter of a shipping magnate. But he's never forgiven himself for the way he left her—and fifteen years later, he's determined to win her back.

Though the attraction is still there, Helena is hesitant to get involved. Nick left her once...what's to stop him from doing it again?

# COMING NEXT MONTH

### #351 IF HE ONLY KNEW... Debbi Rawlins
*Men To Do*

At Sara Wells's impromptu farewell party, coworker Cody Shea gives her a sizzling and unexpected kiss. Now, he may think this is the end, but given the hidden fantasies Sara's always had about the hot Manhattan litigator, this could be the beginning of a long goodbye....

### #352 MY FRONT PAGE SCANDAL Carrie Alexander
*The Martini Dares, Bk. 2*

Bad boy David Carrera is the catalyst Brooke Winfield needs to release her inner wild child. His daring makes her throw off her conservative upbringing...not to mention her clothes. But will she still feel that way when their sexy exploits become front-page news?

### #353 FLYBOY Karen Foley

*A secret corporate club that promotes men who get down and dirty on business travel?* Once aerospace engineer Sedona Stewart finds out why she isn't being promoted, she's ready to quit. But then she's assigned to work with sexy fighter pilot Angel Torres. And suddenly she's tempted to get a little down and dirty herself....

### #354 SHOCK WAVES Colleen Collins
*Sex on the Beach, Bk. 2*

A makeover isn't exactly what Ellie Rockwell planned for her beach vacation. But losing her goth-girl look lands her a spot on her favorite TV show...and the eye of her teenage crush Bill Romero. Now that they're both adults, there's no end to the fun they can have.

### #355 COLD CASE, HOT BODIES Jule McBride
*The Wrong Bed*

Start with a drop-dead-gorgeous cop and a heroine linked to an old murder case. Add a haunted town house in the Five Points area of New York City, and it equals a supremely sexy game of cat and mouse for Dario Donato and Cassidy Case. But their staying one step ahead of the killer seems less dangerous than the scorching heat between them!

### #356 FOR LUST OR MONEY Kate Hoffmann
*Million Dollar Secrets, Bk. 4*

One minute thirty-five-year-old actress Kelly Castelle is pretty well washed-up. The next she's in a new city with all kinds of prospects—and an incredibly hot guy in her bed. Zach Haas is sexy, adventurous...and twenty-four years old. The affair is everything she's ever dreamed about. Only, dreams aren't meant to last....